BECOMING HERSELF

MAUREEN REID

To Russ because of everything

CONTENTS

BEGINNINGS

This letter unleashed a flood of memories buried inside my heart. It was written when I was only child, just 6. I am now almost 25. More than 19 years have passed. When I discovered it, the world went dark. I simply couldn't breathe.

February 1896

Dearest Maggie,

I am not sure if you will ever read this letter, but I write it out of respect for your parents, particularly your beloved Ma.

You are too young to remember what came to pass on the journey we are on, yet you should know what happened these past days. My name is Kathleen Quinn, and my two children and I are on this voyage to America with you and your family. I was with your Ma when she took her last breath and went to the Lord. It happened on our eighth day at sea in late January 1896.

Your Ma was with child but it was early on. She was having a difficult time eating and could barely sip water. She told me the doctor back home in Cork had cautioned her about having another child; her body was too worn-out to stand yet another birthing. She had lost four, two as wee babes and two before they took their first breath. It was a warning she kept from your Da.

I come from Wexford not Cork, so I can't comment on your life there. What I learned from your Ma was that your Da was a carpenter, and a very good one. There was some kind of falling out between him and the bosses on one of the ships he was building and he was having trouble finding work. He had a cousin in New York City that wrote to him about the opportunities for work on all the buildings going up there. He and your Ma thought you would all be better off leaving Ireland and coming to America.

Your older brother James is living in Dublin with your Ma's sister Hannah and her husband, who is a successful businessman. Your Aunt Hannah doesn't have children of her own and since James is better with numbers than with his hands, the decision was made for him to live with them and get a proper education. Your Ma gave me their address to let them know that she had been taken ill. I will put it at the end of this note.

It was our sixth day at sea when your Ma became very ill. Your Da had been trying to get her to eat but she could no longer keep food down. Her fever pitched and your Da was trying to soothe her by putting cool rags on her forehead. Nothing seemed to help. She asked him to get me and one of the other women to come to her. I think she realized that her time was short. Calmly, she asked me to write you a letter. She wanted you to know that she would always love and be with you, even if you couldn't see her.

She was a woman of faith, and although she couldn't understand why God was making her leave you so soon, she accepted his will. Her soul was reflected in her eyes: trusting, true and as aqua blue as the waters of the lakes of the land we were leaving behind.

The following morning, she asked to have you and Nell come to her; she always called you Maggie. She took your hands and had you say your morning prayers with her. Although weak, she clutched both of you in her arms until she was too weary to hold on. As you left her bedside, she told you how much she loved you and how you were to be the big sister to little Nell.

You seemed to sense that something was wrong and kept asking why you had to be sent away. No one answered you. One of the younger women took you by the hand and brought you to stay with her family. The day had been bright and beautiful and the seas calm, but an overwhelming sense of sadness prevailed.

Your Da was by her bedside every moment. He held her hands pleading with her not to leave him. He was like an animal in pain. When she took her last breath, I went to him and told him that he needed to leave so we could get her ready for her funeral. He stood up, a towering presence whose eyes were black with rage. The muscles in his face twitched as he pushed me aside, yelling that he was never going to leave. We wanted him to go to you and your sister, and find comfort in your love and presence. He fell back on his knees, his head bonded to your Ma's chest. He simply could not move.

After many hours, he left. We were not quite sure where he was going and our hearts broke to see a man in such grief. The other women and I began to prepare your Ma for the best funeral we could, given our situation and with no priest to be found. We gently bathed her now peaceful body, rubbing her skin with the creams we brought from home. The stench of death was replaced with the sweet bouquet of the lilies of the valley. We intertwined her well-worn rosary beads into those hands now clasped in final prayer and covered her with the cleanest linens we could find. Candles lit, those of us who had come to know her, sat vigil at her side praying that the Lord would welcome this sweet woman and the babe in her womb to His eternal home.

Your Da showed up early that morning smelling of drink and looking as if Satan himself had taken possession of his soul. He brought with him fresh sailcloth that one of the shipmates had given him. He was crying, muttering that, although he was a carpenter, he didn't have the wood to build his beloved Anna a proper casket. We took the sailcloth from him, dressed your Ma in what we thought to be her best frock, and prepared her to be given up to the sea.

It was a small procession that followed your Ma's body that day. The sun was shining brightly, the winds were calm and the waves gentle, reminding all of us of the kind woman we had just come to know.

You and your sister did not come but stayed with the other family. I think it was the right decision, but a difficult one to make. Your father stood in the back—I am not sure he would have any memory of that time, crazed as he was. We said our prayers and the men lifted your Ma's body and gave her to the deep water. A wave came up as if to her greet her and tenderly rocked her away from us as she disappeared from sight.

We came back and found you and Nell playing jacks with the other children. Your Da had still not come to you. I sat down with you both and told you God had called your Ma to join Him. She would not be coming to America with you, but would be looking down on you from heaven all the days of your life.

Nell was confused and started to cry. You looked at me with very sober eyes—so like your Ma's—and asked if you had to go back to Ireland. I said I didn't know what your Da's plans were but now you should say your prayers to God and to your Ma.

You asked if you could sing her a song. So, after all the prayers were said, you sang the *Ave Maria.* It was if the angels had entered our third-class passage. Your voice was beautiful and so strong for such a young thing. I pray the gift of song the Lord has given you will give you peace and comfort in the days and years ahead.

You and Nell stayed with me and the other families for the rest of the journey. Your Da was like a ghost who would appear for moments and then leave without saying a word.

The day before we docked, just as we could begin to see the land before us, your Da came to me and asked that I pack up your belongings. He had bathed, shaved, and his hair combed. This physical presence of a man strong in body was betrayed by the vacant look in his eyes. Eyes that reflected despair, loss and fear.

He told me one of the captain's men—I think it may have been the same sailor that had given him the fresh sailcloth —was from Germany and a Catholic. His sister was a nun who taught at an orphanage for young girls in Buffalo, New York. Your Da said his plan was to take you and Nell there and then move on. He was not going to stay in New York and did not seem to know where he was going next.

I think it is a very hard decision for him, but a practical one.

Your Da loves you and Nell, but he doesn't have the courage to face life without your Ma.

When I packed your satchels, I found this journal in your Ma's bag. It was carefully wrapped, so I believe it must have been a present she got with her leaving. I put this letter and the journal in your satchel along and said a prayer that both may give you comfort.

You and Nell will be in my prayers.

Sincerely,

Kathleen Quinn

James' address:

Michael & Hannah Riordan

14 Ailesbury Road

Dublin, Ireland

It has been over two weeks since I found this letter so carefully tucked into the journal's flap. I had climbed up the steep ladder that grey afternoon, still grieving for the loss of the wonderful people who had adopted me 19 years ago. They had died within months of each other and I was now emptying the house where I had been raised.

I lost all sense of time. Was I sleeping? Was I awake? Was I going insane?

I don't know how long I sat in the attic. The sun was setting as I made my way down the steps, my Ma's journal with its letter clutched in my arms like a babe that needed protection from the world it had just entered.

I am a grown woman now with a husband and children of my own. It wasn't long after Da had left me in the orphanage that I was adopted by a farm couple who raised me with love and affection. I always called them Mother and Father; my original Ma and Da had left me on the journey over and with their leaving, part of me died as well. I have put them aside, concentrating only on who I am today and not what was, or what could have been.

I am now Margaret. I have not been called Maggie since the day I arrived at the orphanage, not yet 7. I am a farmer's wife and a mother whose day-to-day existence is controlled by the seasons and the needs of those who look to me to be clothed and fed. It is not an unhappy life, but one that has not been explored. Until now.

It was after Mother—the woman who brought me into her home and raised me as her own—died that I found the satchel in her attic, covered in dust so thick its brown leather was shades lighter than its original hue. Yet when I stumbled upon it, the satchel looked vaguely familiar, like a childhood toy that you find unexpectedly in a neighbor's yard.

I have a hazy recollection of carrying it with me on the day I arrived in this house, a memory faded with time. Knowing Mother, she simply put it away to be forgotten, just as she wanted me to forget my past and how I came to call this house my home. She would not have opened it; she was not a woman to pry.

And so, after all these many years, my past has abruptly collided with who I am today. I am rocked to the core. I need to remember who I was. Like a quilt in the making, I must carefully stitch all the pieces together, past and present, to make my life whole.

The Maggie captured in this note had been erased from my memory. Reading about my Ma and Da has opened a wound that never healed though its pain has dulled with time. Death and abandonment. Loss of family, loss of identity, loss of self. And over nineteen years ago.

I have re-read the letter so often this past week that I fear its thin brown paper will begin to tear. I plan to write to James, but first I must get my own thoughts in order. I must see the words on paper. I will write in this journal as my Ma might have done. It will be my conduit for the voice I need to have heard, even if I am its only listener.

I have not told Eli, my husband, what I have found or what I intend to do. I fear he would think me foolish for wanting to reconnect the young child that was with the woman I am today. We shall see. It is one day at a time.

The words are coming easily as I put pen to paper. The images of days gone past are like a kaleidoscope of memories competing for their place on the page.

The Journey

I remember leaving Ireland, shortly after completing my first year at school. It is but a vague memory, blurred after all these many years and with so much to recall.

Emotions were raw, and I recollect the feelings more than the specifics. There was a sense of uneasiness. I cannot even imagine what it must have taken to get the four of us ready for such a journey. How do you choose what to take and what to leave behind?

I have a foggy recollection about packing this satchel, proud to have my own case, something to hold onto when everything else was going to be so different. My memories of Ma and Da are but silhouettes. I cannot make out their faces, but it was their presence—the sense that all was going to be all right as long as Nell and I were with them—that stays with me. I remember feeling safe if Da's strong and muscular hands were clasping mine. It's Ma's eyes I remember, for they were so like mine.

I remember going to Ma's bedside on the steamship after she took sick. She was curled up like a child and couldn't sit up without help. That was not the Ma I knew. My Ma knelt ramrod straight leading us in the rosary each evening with eyes closed and her voice strong and clear. The letter from Mrs. Quinn has stoked the fire of that memory.

It has been years since I have thought of that day or that time. I was confused and afraid, though I could hardly have put those feelings into words. I was only a child, not quite seven.

One of the women, with tears streaming down her face, brought us to where Ma lay so that we could say our prayers and our farewells. I was at a loss about what to do. I couldn't find our Da, so there was no one there for me. knew I had to be strong for Nell, I just didn't know how.

The next day, we were told Ma had gone to the Lord. Da was nowhere to be seen.

I remembered Ma's favorite song was the *Ave Maria*, and all I could think to do was to sing it for her. In the room filled with people I had only known for the past few days, I closed my eyes and raised my voice. The other women joined in, and our voices filled the tiny space where we all huddled. It is music, to this day, that gives me strength in times of both joy and sorrow.

I am not sure how much longer we remained on the steamer. When Da finally came to fetch us, he brought no comfort. It may have been hard for him to look at us as both Nell and I share our Ma's eyes.

I make no excuses for how he was coping with his own grief. I have learned each of us has to face loss in our own way. We should not judge another for the path he or she must take.

I can remember the noise and the smells of New York when we came into the Immigration Center at Castle Garden that bore no resemblance to any garden that I had ever seen. The waft of rotting fish filled the air with toxic fumes. Vendors with their pushcarts and newspaper ragamuffins shouted in strange accents, creating a cacophony of sounds that defied orchestration.

Da led the way, carrying only our satchels. I held on to Nell, who was frightened by the commotion surrounding us. Jostling through the crowd, we found our way to the Grand Central Depot and boarded the train that took us to Buffalo. Da had little to say, and my job was to keep Nell as quiet as possible.

It was my first train ride, and despite all that was going on and all that I didn't understand, I was quite thrilled. To this day, I still love looking out of the window as the train passes through the villages and farms along its journey. My imagination then and now creates stories about the people passing by: who they are, how they live, what they dream. And then my pragmatic side takes over and I simply wonder why the tracks follow this path.

I didn't believe we looked so terribly different than the other passengers on the train, though, in retrospect, we must have been quite a sight: a grown man, eyes vacant and lost, with two youngsters who were in desperate need of a hot bath and a good hair brush.

The Orphanage

I vaguely remember taking a carriage from the train station. It was a windy day, and the cold seeped through my every pore. The air whipped ice pelts at our faces while the horses navigated the rutted roads of this strange and bustling City I now know so well. Da had tried to fix my raven hair and put it in braids as Ma had always done, but it was unruly and wouldn't cooperate. He just let it go wild, stuffing it under my well-worn cap. It was good to have his attention, even for the moment.

Nell needed no preening. Her hair fell in soft auburn curls, framing porcelain skin and the blue-green eyes we shared. She was always labeled the beauty, and I was the one they called smart, sometimes "too smart for her own good."

An imposing red brick building with few trees and an austere, no-nonsense look was our destination. Da had not said a word as to where we were going or what we would be doing next. Nell and I said nothing. For once she didn't complain that I was holding her too tight, for my tight grip provided both the needed warmth and comfort.

As we got out of the carriage, he took our satchels and told the driver to wait. I cannot remember what I was thinking at that moment. Everything was coming too quickly, and without Ma, there was no one to shelter and guide us.

A long cobblestone walk led up to the door. Nell's legs couldn't stretch to make the steps, so Da had to carry her. Two nuns answered his knock, and he entered, while Nell and I stayed outside and waited. After a few minutes, he returned, kissed us quickly on the cheeks, and told us to be good girls. I never saw him again.

We had been placed in the Orphanage for German Girls.

One of the nuns, Sister Gabrielle, was kind as I tried to get my bearings. Looking back, she must have been quite young. I asked, *What has happened—why are we here? Where is my Da going? Do you know my Ma is in heaven? My name is Maggie and this is my sister Nell. I am older by almost 3 years.*

She kissed the top of my head and said it was in God's plan that we were to stay at the orphanage. And we should pray each day to find another family that would love us. I started to cry, and Nell asked why I was sad. I stopped crying then. I knew I had to be strong for Nell.

I took Nell's hand and told her she didn't need any other family; she had me. Sister Gabrielle smiled: *We shall call you Margaret, for there is no saint called Maggie. And while I love your accent, there may be others here who will have a hard time understanding you. We will need to change that.*

I remember thinking no one had ever told me I had an accent, and I wasn't quite sure what it meant. I asked Sister Gabrielle if Nell had one, too.

Nell is young, and she has just begun to talk; it won't be hard for her to learn the new ways. You, on the other hand, will need to work harder. It will be the only way for you to get adopted. No one wants an Irish scrub mop in their fine house.

I wasn't quite sure what a "scrub mop" was, but decided I had asked enough questions.

Sister Gabrielle showed us through the orphanage, a huge

four-story building. The girls' dormitory on the third floor—a series of cots in one of the large rooms—was our destination. Nell and I were to be separated, as she was to be put in the younger girls' smaller room. I asked Sister to have her sleep with me, since we had never been away from each other. She agreed, but only for the first night.

The other girls stared at us as we went to my assigned cot. No one said anything, and I soon learned that was the rule when the nuns were present. I didn't want to talk anyway, now that I knew I was afflicted with something called "an accent." Better to keep silent, though that has never been my natural inclination.

Sister gave us our clothes. All the girls wore the same gray dresses with white aprons during the day and a night shirt to bed. She took our satchels and said they would be returned to us when the day came that we left the orphanage.

There were no lights in the room, but the sun was not yet down. We were told to get on our knees and say our evening prayers. I closed my eyes but the words wouldn't come. I was numb with fear and exhaustion. I was going through the motions with no sense of where I was or what I was doing. Then we went to bed.

Nell complained she was hungry—Da had given us breakfast on the train, but we hadn't had anything to eat since. I was too nervous to even thinking about food but that never stopped Nell. I told her we should pretend to eat and began to describe the great feast being prepared for us. We cuddled in the small space as I whispered in her ear. As her eyes began to close, I kissed her nose. It was always our joke that my kisses kept her freckles from leaving her nose and spreading all over her face.

I don't know why this memory is so clear to me now. Perhaps because it was the last time I fell asleep with Nell in my arms.

The next day, the bell rang early, and all the girls jumped out of bed and fell on their knees to say their morning prayers. I looked around to find a room full of girls about my age who threw sly glances my way. No one smiled or offered any warm greetings. I held Nell close to me as I watched the daily ritual begin.

We made up our cot and marched in an orderly procession to breakfast. Still no one spoke to me. Sister Gabrielle came to fetch Nell, who in true Nell form boldly shook her curls and pronounced that she couldn't leave as she hadn't yet had her porridge. Sister Gabrielle smiled and reassured her that a bowl of porridge was soon to be had.

I was given my tasks: cleaning the pots and pans in the kitchen. I was shown my way into the kitchen and to the sink where the remnants of the day's porridge was to be removed so that the evening soup could start to simmer. It felt good to be doing something. I had the same chores at home, so I was on familiar turf.

After our morning tasks, we went into the classroom and started our lessons. Here was where I wanted to be. I was never happier than when I was given a slate with chalk. I had not been in school in months and missed every aspect of it. In Ireland, I had learned the basics and Ma had encouraged us in our reading and sums. Now I was back in a classroom. I was like a sponge, soaking up information, reading all I could.

Reluctant to raise my hand to speak, I searched for the answers myself. A habit that continues to serve me well.

And our daily pattern commenced—a routine that would not be broken, except on Sundays, when, after Mass, there would be more play time and meat for dinner.

Those early days were filled with the relief of routine. It was at night, alone in the cot that the emptiness found me. I longed for my Ma's touch, her gentle ways, her sweet voice calling my name. I dreamt, often fitfully. Once I even saw Ma at the side of my cot. She looked healthy and happy, not as I remembered her on that ship. I reached out to touch her but she gently shook her head. *I love you Maggie. I will always be with you. When you sing, I will hear your voice. Forgive Da. He did the best he could.* And a tear fell from her eye. *Be brave.* Then she was gone. I woke up, shocked to see I was still in the orphanage, still alone. But I had Nell and I knew that Ma would always be with me. That seemed enough for the moment.

I still can feel Ma's presence though I cannot remember her face. And even today, that brings a sadness that seeps through my very being.

Our first Sunday at the orphanage, we marched single file into the chapel, and the nun who had talked with Da clicked her rosary crucifix on the first wooden pew. Each of us dropped to our knees. Another click and we rose and moved silently into our pews.

During the Mass, the organ started to play the *Panis Angelicus.* This is still one of my favorite hymns, and I sang out in full voice. It felt wonderful to be hearing music and feel a part of the song. I lost all sense of where I was. The music filled me and I was at peace for that moment.

Later Sister Gabrielle came up to me in the playground. She told me I had a beautiful voice and my accent was lost when I sang. I was to join the choir. By now, I figured out my "accent" labeled me as Irish and that was not a good thing. I was to lose it should I want to be adopted or at least accepted in this new world.

The good news was, from that day on, I was to spend an hour a day practicing with the choir. The other nuns were welcoming, as were the few other girls who were part of the group. Listening to how they spoke, I could hear how different my voice was. I had a lilt, and I knew I had to work hard to change it.

Those first few weeks, Nell and I saw each other during play period. Her sweet disposition had charmed the nuns, and she had quickly become a favorite. Given my position in the choir and Nell's role as the nuns' pet, our life was not what we would have chosen, but we were not unhappy. The other girls accepted us well enough though I kept my distance. My accent was still a barrier and I had Nell. That was enough at least until about the third month into our stay.

Nell came bustling into the playground to find me. *Maggie, I am moving to Philadelphia with a beautiful lady who lives in a big house and is going to buy me dresses.* Flushed with excitement, she held out a porcelain doll dressed in the finest fabric: *My new doll is going with me.*

My stomach turned over and my vision blurred. Nell was being adopted and leaving the orphanage. Leaving me. The cloudless blue sky mocked me with the beauty of the day. Just when I thought I could survive in this new world, I was tossed backward. Nell was moving to Philadelphia, a place I had not even heard about and wondered if it was even in America. I took her in my arms and hugged with all the strength I could muster.

You need to be a good girl always. Remember to pray to our Ma and never forget me. Her aqua eyes, so like mine, turned solemn and filled with tears. I told her I loved her, kissed her on her nose, and walked to the other edge of playground.

In the corner of my eye, I saw a young couple, better dressed than any I had ever seen. They took Nell's hand and placed her between them in a four-in-hand carriage with matched horses.

It was the last time I ever saw her. I stared at the fence that kept us apart from the world as her carriage pulled away and disappeared.

In four months' time, I had left my home, lost my Ma, and had been abandoned by my Da. Now Nell was gone, too. Tears fell down my face and I could barely catch my breath. I was alone in the world. I would need to make my own way

It was the last time I cried.

Those first few days after Nell left were dark. Without her, I had no sense of purpose, no moral compass. I didn't know where I was or where I belonged. I lashed out at the world around me.

Given my place in the choir, the scoldings I received paled in comparison to the other girls' whose beds were not made wrinkle-free or whose noses turned up at the sight of the watery broth being passed as our evening stew.

It was my defense of the next newest girl, Maria, which got me the worst punishment I received.

I was still assigned the kitchen duties, but I had worked my way from the pots and pans to washing and cleaning the glasses and plates, a marked improvement in my daily chores. Maria had just arrived, and she and I shared nothing in common. Her parents were both alive, but with six other children, they brought her to the orphanage, along with her brother, Will.

She was told her parents were planning to come back for her. But even at eight, Maria was realistic about life and all its options. *They can't feed what they have and they just keep having more of us*, she shrugged.

In the kitchen, one of the older girls, Greta, who was always scowling, even during play periods, was in charge of us. She began to single out Maria for ridicule from the first day. Perhaps it was because she had to leave me alone due to my standing in the choir that her vengeance on Maria was so acute. For whatever reason, and given my sense of loss, I could not tolerate the perceived injustice of it all.

On our fourth day together, Greta again threw a large pot back at Maria, soaking her and the floor, screaming it had not been scrubbed clean and that Maria was lazy and stupid. Without thinking, I rushed over to Greta and pushed Maria out of the way. *You are no Christian girl*, I screamed.

You are nothing but a poor Mick that doesn't even talk right, Greta shouted back. *Your hair flies all over the place, like it was looking for a new home. Who would want to be stuck with the likes of you all day?*

And though she had me by a few inches, I threw myself at her. Before I knew it, we were on the ground, pulling each other's hair and throwing punches. I remembered well the fisticuffs roughhousing with my brother in Ireland and was well on my way to winning the match when Sister Gabrielle walked in.

Needless to say, I was labeled the culprit, a role I quickly acknowledged. The other girls were dismissed, and I was told to go the chapel to pray to be forgiven. There would be no lunch or dinner for me that evening. And I was to apologize to Greta.

The first part of the punishment seemed just. The second— the apology—seemed more than I could muster.

Even though my explanations about Greta's treatment of Maria and the insults she had hurled at me seemed to justify my actions, Sister would have none of it. *You are responsible for creating a disturbance in the orphanage, Margaret. We will have none of that. Not today, not tomorrow. In the morning, after your day of repentance, you are to say you are sorry to Greta. I will be present to be sure she accepts your apology. Now go to chapel. I will explain why you are not at choir practice today.*

That night, I crawled into bed, knees aching after spending so many hours on them, and stomach rumbling from lack of food. Lo and behold! Under my pillow—discretely hidden— was a piece of bread with a bit of butter. I looked over at Maria who simply winked at me and rolled over.

The next day when Sister Gabrielle escorted me into the

kitchen to do my penance, it was Maria who was by my side. The other girls looked sheepish as I apologized to Greta but Maria kept her eyes focused solely on Greta. With the task done, and Greta acknowledging my remorse, we returned to our chores. The next day Greta was reassigned to duties other than the kitchen. Our nemesis had been removed and it all seemed to have turned out just fine.

From that day on, Maria and I became inseparable. We would share our school books and read stories to each other. Maria would correct me if I used the wrong phase or gently ask me to repeat myself if my accent was too pronounced. If I had questions about something we were reading and Maria didn't have the answer, it would be Maria that would ask the question next day in class. It was an arrangement that worked well for each of us.

Although far too young to understand what it meant to have a vocation, Maria and I decided we would take the veil. We would become nuns and live together always. It was good to have a plan. It was good to feel safe. There was security within the walls of the orphanage.

Our biggest concern as we contemplated this next step was our hair. Maria's ebony braids were thick and lustrous; my raven locks fell every which way, seeming to have a mind of their own. Yet they were such a part of us. We agreed that cutting our hair might change this plan of ours. But first, we needed to find out what the nuns' hair looked like behind the veil.

Our attempt to sneak into the convent and peek at the nuns while they lay sleeping in their cots was a failure.

We assumed they slept in the same large room and on the same beds as we did, merely larger versions. As best we could, we mapped out the hallways, finding the path from kitchen to the convent dining room that we deemed to be our best route.

One Sunday afternoon, thinking we were the cleverest of spies, off on our clandestine journey we went. Hearts beating quickly, we found the doors locked.

All of a sudden we heard the rustling of robes; the nuns were on their way out the very door we were so valiantly attempting to unlock. Palms sweating, we unglued ourselves from the wall that we had been pressed against and scrambled back quickly before our adventure became a misadventure. I had no desire to spend another day in supplication.

We then decided it might be simpler to ask Sister Gabrielle.

The next week, with all the courage we could muster, Maria and I asked if we could speak with her confidentially. She ushered us into the empty classroom and cautiously inquired as to what the great concern could be.

We told of our plan to become nuns and our great concern about our hair. What was to become of it?

Sister Gabrielle broke out in a mischievous grin. *I am tempted to tell you that we all have feathers and ribbons under our veils, but that would be silly. All of the nuns here at the orphanage have hair—of all different lengths and colors. We cut each other's hair, and it is a good thing we can follow a straight line so as not to cut our ears off!*

The conversation then took a more serious tone. *Margaret and Maria, devoting your life to God is not just about having to decide whether or not to cut your hair. I thought I would follow the same track as my mother and sisters: meeting someone, marrying, having children. But that is not the path God had for me. When you enter the convent, you make a decision to surrender your life to God. That is a very big decision and one you should never take lightly.*

I live in a religious community where our lives are dedicated to prayer. All of the sisters are committed to teaching, healing, and servicing others. So, when the time comes, my children, you will need to think through all your choices. Just as I did. For now, go back to your lessons and prepare for your classes.

With that, we were dismissed. Maria and I agreed we had time before we had to contemplate taking our vows. But if we could spend the rest of our lives with Sister Gabrielle, that would be good indeed.

That Christmas, the nuns opened the orphanage doors to the public to hear the pageant we had been preparing. Thinking back, it must have been their way to introduce their orphans to potential parents, couples shopping for a child or an extra pair of hands.

Our clothes were freshly pressed, and we were as spic and span as the parlor floor. I was quite excited as I had a solo. I had been practicing *Adeste Fideles* to try and remove any trace of my accent in the hymn.

The main hallway was decorated with a giant Christmas tree lit with real candles. It was a wonder we didn't all go up in flames. Little did I know then that putting candles on a tree was going to be part of my holiday celebrations for years to come.

The program was a great success. The sounds of the choir resonated throughout the Chapel. Maria gave me a quick wink as I stepped forward to begin my solo. I briefly nodded as I closed my eyes and raised my voice in song. When I was done, I stepped back into my place in the choir and Sister Gabrielle gave me a slight smile. I thought my heart would burst. I hadn't been that happy in such a very long time.

The afternoon following the performance, one of the nuns came to me and said a Mr. and Mrs. Meyer wanted to meet me. I was to wash up, try to put my hair in order and come into the parlor. The washing up was easy, but my hair escaped its tightly braided coils, no matter how hard I tried to keep it all in place. I shrugged my shoulders recognizing this was the best I could muster, and made my way downstairs, heart pounding and palms sweating.

It is funny what I recall from seeing them the first time. They were seated stiffly, with their eyes seemingly unblinking. The nun who had met me and Nell on our first day was talking with them.

Mrs. Meyer seemed much bigger than Mr. Meyer as they rose to meet me, though she was only an inch or two taller. Though neither particularly big nor stout, she simply filled the space she was in by the sheer force of being her.

It was her eyes that captivated you. They were not brilliant in color but were intelligent and kind. I remember looking straight into them when she pulled the chair over to talk with me. It was if those eyes could see into my soul. Unlike Ma, she exuded health.

Her fingers entwined with mine were thick and muscular. They were covered with lovely crocheted gloves, open at the fingertips. I later learned that her hands—she used the phase, *Wäschemagd* hands—embarrassed her, and she looked to cover them whenever she could.

Mr. Meyer seemed foreboding. He had a huge mustache waxed to a perfect curl at its tips. I had never seen anything quite like it before, and remembering I shouldn't stare, averted my eyes downward.

I got such a surprise, for then I noticed his shoes. He was wearing spats—fawn-colored with buttons at the sides that were fastened under the foot of his shoes with a buckled strap. I later learned he got them for his wedding day. He kept them in their original box and wore them on special occasions, his one and only vanity.

The conversation began with the simple statement: *Come Margaret, tell us about yourself.*

For the first time in my life, I could think of nothing to say. I think I blurted out I was Irish but was trying to lose my accent. I said that I worked hard at my studies but I didn't ask a lot of questions as I didn't want the other girls to make fun of me. I told her that my Ma was in heaven and that I pray for her and my little sister Nell, who is now living with her new parents in some place called Philadelphia. I asked if she knew where that was, and Mr. Meyer replied, *Yes, but a very great distance.* Mrs. Meyer asked how I felt when I sing, I told her that it is if the angels filled my soul and let themselves out in my voice. She smiled.

Soon I was given my satchel, and the doors of the orphanage closed shut behind me.

I never said good-bye to Maria; I never even knew her last name. I was but one other person who had abandoned her. It brought back to me how I felt when Da left us and never looked back. Alone. Deserted. Sad. Scared.

Now I had done the same. But there was no choice. Perhaps it was the same for Da, though I will never know. Over the years, I have forgiven him, and that nagging pain is a distant memory. Perhaps, or at least I hope, Maria has forgiven me as well.

It has been years since I thought of her. I pray she is well.

I never went back to the orphanage. I was to be a farmer's daughter, a role I knew I had to take on with all the energy and fervor I could muster. I no longer had my own family and these new people said they wanted me. I tried to look happy as I realized all I had ever known was gone for good. There was no Ma, no Da, no Nell. Only me. And now a Mr. and Mrs. Meyer whom I was to call Father and Mother. I would not, could not, let my longing for what was destroy any chance I had for future happiness.

Even as a child, I knew that.

My life in Ireland became, in my mind, my 'before life'. As the years progressed, my memories of those early years dimmed and the ache for what was or what could have been faded.

Until now.

A New Life

I can remember the first time I saw the house that would be my new home, the house I am now closing down and turning over to others to call their own.

It was a long journey, particularly on an Arctic-cold day. Though I had seen snow before, on the playground and on the sidewalks in front of the orphanage, I had never seen such masses of it. It was two hours since we left, and the further east we traveled, the more the world became transformed, as if all around us was blanketed in a white coverlet.

As our journey continued, there was no wind, and even the air smelled cold, burning my nostrils if I took too deep a breath. And it was clean. The smoke and grit of Cork and Buffalo were far behind me. This was open farmland. The skies were clear, and as the sun went down, there were too many stars to count and the moon so bright it was our own private lantern.

I thought of Cork with its houses jammed so close to one another that you could hear a neighbor talking, even when they preferred you didn't. And its smoked-filled skies that caused too many to cough too loudly and die too soon.

I was quiet on the carriage ride as I lay covered with thick wool blankets that kept me still and warm. I was nestled between this man and woman I would call Father and Mother. I knew they would be never be my Ma and Da, but that chapter in my life was over. I had my eyes closed, pretending to sleep rather than letting the world know I was so scared that my lunch was roaring around in my stomach, threatening to reappear.

I heard Father ask Mother if she was sure it was me she wanted. Father had a German accent similar to the nuns in the orphanage, so I accustomed to the rhythm of his speech. Mother must have said the words to reassure him: *When she sings, it sounds as if choirs of angels are nearby.*

I remember thinking I would need to remind myself to keep in good voice and mind my manners. One of the older girls had told me if my new parents didn't like me, the nuns at the orphanage wouldn't take me back. I would be put in an institution for unloved children and be penniless my whole life. My nearly 7-year old imagination took over with vivid images of living in destitution. I wasn't sure what my life was going to be, but silently vowed I would try to be the girl the Meyers wanted to keep. I did not want to be tossed back.

Sheldon, New York

Three hours after we began, we arrived in Sheldon, my new home. It was smaller than any of the small towns I had visited in Ireland. Two churches, a school house, a gray shingled store marking the crossroads. I had not felt this alone since the day Nell left the orphanage all those many months ago.

In the past 19 years, not much has changed except it is now my village and the small store has grown in size and painted a bright yellow. A gas station is in the process of being built, a sure sign that the modern age is upon us.

It is hard to explain the comfort a small town brings and how it also suffocates. You know its every nook and cranny—what apple trees bloom brightest in spring and how the first signs of autumn leave their mark on the same branches. You know everyone by their first name and when they were born.

Most are related, the shirt-tail relations forging ties from so long ago they are still potential suitors. You were present when most of the young ones came into this world, and you nurse and bring comfort to those who are leaving it. Only the darkest secrets can be hidden.

These are the neighbors who come to help you harvest, who visit on Sundays, who bring you dinner to feed your family when you are too weak from having given birth to yet another child. You pray with them. You laugh with them. You count on them. And they on you.

Yet there are times when it all seems just too small, when the predictability of the seasons and the same story told yet again make you want to scream. At these times, the walls seem to be crashing in all around you. You don't want the sun to rise in the east. You want to do more, see more, think about something different.

But that is not what you do in a small town. That is not what you do in Sheldon.

Mother and Father

From that day on, I was Margaret Meyer, the daughter of Elizabeth and John Meyer. Maggie Clancy ceased to exist, and everyone—me included—worked hard to keep her far away, like an unwelcomed relative you would prefer not to invite for Sunday dinner.

Mother was wonderful to me from the day I arrived until she left this world, just three months ago. I believe God hadn't given her the blessing of her own children so that she could guide and care for me. She was a strong woman with a heart so full of love for others that I ache knowing she has left me.

From the age of almost 7 and through the years she nurtured me, I never heard her say an unkind word about anyone. When I came home from school or from an outing with friends with a litany of wrongs imposed upon me or tales that I couldn't wait to tattle, she would merely smile and say, *Not now, Margaret. Let us finds something pleasant to talk about, and then later we can get back to these disagreeable topics.*

Somehow, we never did.

The church was her anchor, her faith sustained her through countless miscarriages and three stillborn births. She was not angry at God. *The Lord has his reason in all things, Margaret. You must always remember that.* Thinking back, she might have been trying to help me better understand why my family had been taken away from me at such an early age, a topic we simply never discussed.

Father was stern, but never mean. He had been born in Germany and immigrated to New York when he was a young boy. His strong German accent made him reluctant to speak to strangers.

Though born in America, Mother's family also had German roots, so there were times they would speak in the "old language." I always believed I was the topic of these conversations.

As an only child of a successful farmer, I wanted for very

little, and there was very little we needed. The farm provided for all our basic needs. The cows and chickens did their bit. Father saw to that. Mother had her garden. We hoed, weeded and tended the vegetables throughout the spring and summer. After the savage winters that batter upstate New York, I embraced the long-awaited summer sun as a welcomed visitor. Its warmth brought beads of perspiration all over my body, as if I had been sprinkled with heated water.

In the autumn, we harvested, canned and filled the root cellar in preparation for the winter months ahead. It was and is hard, but not unwelcome, work.

There is a rhythm to the seasons of being a farmer that brings peace to the soul. I found it when I arrived all those many years ago. I feel it still today.

Being bound to the earth is a good thing, a covenant with nature. There is a respect for the land and for all living things: the horses that pull our wagons, the chickens that lay our eggs, the cows that provide us milk. We could not live without them. And they could not survive without us.

I believe God intended all living things to exist in harmony. And it is on a farm that you can hear His symphony played each day in the fields, barns and gardens.

Christmas 1896

This was the first Christmas that I was not in Ireland. This was my new home, this was my new family. This is how my holidays were to be celebrated from that time on. Mother and Father took me to Christmas Eve Mass as my initial venture outside the house about a week after I had arrived. It was the first time I was to see the church that continues to play such an important part in my life.

To this day, I am not sure where Mother found a warm coat for me. I can still see it: gray with pearl buttons. And though I was tall for my age, it must have been sizes too big. I thought it was the grandest thing I had ever worn. I remember asking if it were mine or a "borrow." Mother assured me it was mine and that it would look more fitting once she took her needle and thread to it.

During the service, I took my place between Mother and Father and made sure I kept my eyes on the altar and my hands folded in prayer throughout the Mass. Thanks to the nuns at the orphanage, I knew when to raise my eyes and properly bow my head. Mother cautioned me not to speak to anyone, and to merely smile when introduced. I knew my accent was the issue. It was hard not to sing the carols that I knew, but I understood the time to raise my voice in song was yet to come.

As we left the church that evening, snowflakes were drifting to the ground. The sky was crystal clear, and the moon so big it looked like the sun had a found a twin to take its place in the night sky. I thought of Ma. She was up there somewhere looking down at me and smiling. She had brought me to a good place. These were good people. I would be safe. The next morning was Christmas Day. As I slowly came into the parlor, I gasped in sheer delight. Balsamic fir wreaths dressed in pine cones and red ribbons filled the house. Mother had been up baking and the smell of pine was mixed with the aroma of cinnamon and brown sugar. To this day, it is that bouquet that makes me think Christmas. I had never seen anything like this before. And then I spotted it—three stockings were hung by the fireplace mantle. I was wide-eyed with wonder as Father handed one to me.

I had my very own stocking and tucked inside were an orange and a doll. I had never had such treasures. An abundance of riches.

I took the doll in my arms; it was made of cloth, with a bright blue dress. Thinking back, Mother had a dress of the same fabric, but I was too wonderstruck to make that connection. The doll had button eyes with a mouth and eyebrows embroidered with the finest stitches. She was, by far, the most beautiful doll I had ever seen, and she was mine. To hold and to love. I would not have to sleep alone again.

Naturally, I called her "Nell," and from that moment on, we became inseparable. My dreams were often dark, memories of what was lost and what could have been disturbed my sleep. When I woke up frightened and confused, I would search for my new Nell and my fears would subside. This Nell bridged my old and new worlds. She became my comfort and my strength. Again and again, the yellow yarn hair would be replaced and the muslin legs and arms re-sewn. Nell was my confidante and my talisman.

In the years that followed, when I lacked courage to move forward, it was Nell who heard my fears before I took the next step. And only on this page can I confess that I even slipped her in the bag that was packed for my honeymoon night, just in case she was needed. Yes, this Nell has always been there for me.

I pray that my little sister Nell has found a Margaret to hold onto as she navigates the twists and turns in her new life. It is only in my dreams I see her and while I now know where Philadelphia is, she is lost to me. I know we shall never meet again. The orphanage kept no records and no one ever told me the name of the couple that took Nell home with them.

Back to that first Christmas Day, and the orange. I simply had never seen one. I didn't even know what one was to do with it. Toss it? Roll it on the floor? Was it a strange toy? And the color! Given its inglorious past, the color orange is not necessarily a hue the Irish are prone to embrace.

Mother must have sensed my bewilderment because she asked: *Do you know what this is, Margaret?* When I shook my head no, she gave that knowing smile and nodded to Father. *It is an orange. A delight to enjoy anytime of the year. But a special treat at Christmas. Father will show you how to eat it.*

With the gravity the Founding Fathers must have felt when signing the Declaration, Father extracted the pen knife from his pocket. With the precision of the butcher he was, he cut away the nubby, bright skin. Beneath the bumpy exterior lay slices ready to be eaten. As if presenting the royal jewels, he handed me one and told me to take a bite.

My eyes must have jumped out of my head. Never had I tasted anything like this! Sweet and tart. Juice and pulp. I wanted to eat it all at once. I wanted to hoard it, to take only the smallest bite each day so it would last forever. I didn't know what to do now that I had tasted this most wonderful of treats

Father smiled. *Mother and I will help you finish this, Margaret.*

We have two more we can share later this week. It is our Christmas tradition.

And that is how this family began with a fire roaring, fresh rolls baking, sharing this rare delicacy called an orange. Once it was finished, we laughed together as we wiped the juice from our mouths, Mother picked up the orange peels. *We will grind these up to use as sachets for gifts for our friends when we go call. Waste not, Want not.*

It would be the mantra that set the pace of our daily life on the farm.

The Bavarian Family Secret Sachet

It was part of our family folklore that, upon arriving, I was convinced winter would never leave Sheldon. I told Mother as much about four weeks into my arrival, when the world all around us was still covered in snow. Supposedly, I asked if she had ever seen a garden.

And then the magic began.

Mother disappeared into the root cellar, the spot I had not yet mustered enough courage to explore. She descended down its dark, deep stairs while my not quite seven-year-old imagination conjured up all sorts of demons and diabolical creatures lurking in its every corner. I was convinced a young Irish girl was just the morsel they hoped to devour, given the chance.

I peered cautiously around the corner as Mother's skirts swooped down the dirt steps. Soon, much to my relief, her silhouette appeared in the dimming daylight.

In her arms, she carried myriad treasures, swaddled in the thinnest of tissue paper. She presented her riches to me with reverence the Magi must have displayed when presenting their gifts to the infant Jesus. Dried flowers and herbs. Oils in small glass jars. Smells I remember to this day, so strong and fragrant our kitchen was soon overpowered with the most exotic aromas. I got quite giddy.

And then she told the story of Ma Grande Tante's Qui Sent Bonne.

We are going to make my family's famous sachet, Margaret. My Great Aunt Madeleine came from Paris and was a personal maid to a wealthy lady. She married my grandmother's brother, Leon. Their love affair caused quite the scandal, since they eloped in the dead of night.

The two had met one afternoon as Leon was coming out of the famous Cathedral of Notre Dame, where he had gone to pray to the Virgin for his safe return to Bavaria. He had been taken from his home against his will to serve in the French King's army.

Madeleine was quite taken by his thick dark hair and intrigued by this soldier who prayed to Our Lady. She agreed to walk with him along the river Seine as it twisted and turned its way through the bustling city. By the time they had finished the stroll, they had fallen madly in love.

Three days later Madeleine climbed down the cherry tree outside her window and fell into his arms. Leon escaped his regiment and they were off on this most remarkable adventure. Their arrival five days later at his parents' house in Bavaria caused such uproar.

Mother chuckled as she put the kettle on to make another cup of tea and continued their story.

You see, Margaret, good girls, even in those days, guarded their good names and reputation. I trust you will do the same.

Anyway, the priest was called, the vows were exchanged, and Madeleine and Leon were wed in the eyes of the Church.

My grandparents had already booked passage to come to America to start their life here. My grandfather was the fourth son and would never inherit a farm of his own. So, Leon and Madeleine joined the party, and off the two couples ventured to this new land, looking for opportunities and a new beginning.

They arrived in Sheldon where others from their village had settled. From that day on, everyone lived under the same roof, which they shared with their precious livestock. Leon and Madeleine had no children, and my beloved Mother, as the only daughter, was raised by both these women while their husbands labored in the fields

I couldn't help myself, I had to interrupt the story. *They lived with the animals, like in a barn?* Mother smiled, not the least disturbed by the interruption. *Yes, Margaret, in those days farmers had few comforts and lived with their livestock under the same roof for protection. We have come a long way since those days and have much to be thankful for.*

And she continued, *It was Madeleine, her Tante—that is "Aunt" in French—who taught her how to make these wonderful sachets. My own dear Mother always referred to her as my Grand Tante—Great Aunt, and that is how I have named the sachets.*

Mother showed me four glass containers which she clasped

with the utmost reverence. She held them up to the candlelight in the same way the priest holds up the chalice at Mass. Mother looked as though she, too, were making an offering to the Almighty.

It is knowing how to make these oils that makes the difference when we create our sachets. It is our family secret, one that has been passed down to us by Grande Tante Madeleine. We keep this within this family, Margaret. It is not to be shared with others.

We take the dry leaves from the flowers or herbs—whatever you like—to make the sachets themselves. But it is the oils that keep the scents fresh. It is the oils that Grande Tante Madeleine taught us to make.

We bring these sachets when we call on our neighbors, and they are welcomed gifts. Most of the ingredients come from our garden —so yes, we have our garden. Quite the envy of all our neighbors, I might add. But more important, not only does our garden provide us with food and nourishment. It also gives us the ingredients we need to make our secret sachets.

I will teach you how to do all of this. And you will teach your children. It is our tradition, and while others may try to imitate, they are never successful. Why? Because they do not know about our oils.

Tomorrow we will start making the sachets.

The next morning, after our outside chores and the breakfast dishes had been done, Mother looked quite solemn. *Now is the time to make the pouches, Margaret. You must learn how to sew tiny stitches. Delicate at every turn. For that is how the sachet is created. Today, you shall watch.*

The kitchen table's solid wood glistened with the lemon oil that we daily scrubbed into its grains. Mother removed the vestiges of our daily meals and the table took on a new incarnation. On this day, it became the chalkboard for the lesson I was about to learn.

The winter sun was shining through the windowed curtains as I took my place on the high stool next to Mother's chair. The kitchen was transformed before my eyes. The cast-iron stove lost its dominance as the center of our world, replaced by the silver of the needles Mother carefully extracted from their velvet cushion.

Mother nodded silently as the ritual began, her lips turning up in a small smile while her determined eyes flashed with something that must have been streaks of joy. She was passing down a family ritual. Her family's ritual. She had assumed the role of teacher and guide as her mother did before her. Even then, I knew one day I would share the same secret with my daughters as well.

But on that day, my job was to watch. And watch I did.

In a thatched basket filled with cloth, lace, buttons and ribbons, she pulled out bits and pieces. Mother could spin magic with a simple thread and needle. An excess of stitches: the backstitch, slip stitch, whipstitch. And such lovely things she created: each different, unique, one lovelier than the next. As the sun began to fade and the evening shadows danced on the table, Mother smiled. *Now we wait Margaret, when the time is right they will each be filled with Ma Grande Tante's Qui Sent Bonne. I will teach you how to extract the oils and preserve them. You will learn the secret that makes us famous.* And her eyes danced with humor. And as the kerosene lamps were lit,

Mother solemnly packed away these new creations and the kitchen returned to its usual role as the hub of meal preparation and consumption. The magic was gone, but not forgotten.

It was Mother's simple act of sewing that brought to me peace and comfort, and stilled my aching soul. I gazed solemnly as she formed a double loop, tying off the knot, and snipping the tread from the spool with ease and grace. I knew I had much to learn from her.

And I believe it was from that day on I knew I could never disappoint. I must always be the best. This woman trusted me with family secrets. She would teach me to sew. We would make beautiful things. I would become whatever she wanted me to become. I owed her that.

I felt loved and wanted, no longer an abandoned child. No longer alone in the world. This was my new life. From then and until today, I have seldom looked back. The curtain was closed.

Music

Music defines me. It helps me appreciate the lyrical quality of life: words and melodies that move the soul no matter what we look like or how we speak.

For me, music is air. I am not sure I could survive without it. From my earliest memory, I simply sang whenever and wherever I could. I was told my voice was extraordinary—I had a range quite unlike what would be expected of a child my age. I had no idea what any of that meant. I simply opened my mouth, took a deep breath, and sang. To this day, other than the 40 days of Lent when all music stops, not a day goes by that I do not sing.

I sing when I am happy. I sing when I am sad. Sometimes I sing for no reason at all. I just need to sing.

As a soprano with a three-octave range, my voice easily moves between registers, with a pure and clear sound and natural vibrato. I learned all of this when I took over as the head of the choir and had to plan the musical arrangements. Yet from my earliest moments, I would simply open up my mouth and let the music flow. As I think back, which is all I am doing at the moment, it was this gift that eased me into the life I now call mine.

Sheldon winters are harsh. For weeks unending, the trees remain bare, their nests empty of the birds that have wisely flown to warmer climates. The fields are white, with the occasional corn stalk browned from all its waiting, poking its forgotten head through the mound of glazed snow. In those first few months, when no one wanted to venture out and no friends wanted to venture in, Mother spent hours reading with me. Slowly, the lilt that accompanied me across the seas diminished, and I lost all the remnants of "Maggie" and became only "Margaret." Mother and I sang each evening, mainly hymns, her lovely alto voice complementing my soprano. By the time the roads were ready to be traveled without the fear of a sudden squall or ice storm, it was early March, and I was ready for my Sheldon debut.

And what a debut it was.

One evening, Mother announced we were going to choir practice the next afternoon. The roads had been impassable for almost six weeks, and we hadn't been to church since mid-January. Knowing I was now going to join her in choir was both exhilarating and terrifying.

I had sung with the nuns in the orphanage, so I understood the demands I would be facing. But I was not yet part of this community. Other than Mother and Father, in the three months I had lived in Sheldon, I had not spoken a word to anyone else, and I was terrified I would disappoint.

Mother would have none of it.

That first afternoon, Mother simply took her place in the choir loft with me beside her. She engaged in polite chatter with the other women while I kept my head down, avoiding eye contact with any and all.

Although she knew I was nervous, she would not indulge me. No words of encouragement. No holding of my hand. She handed me the hymnal, and Mrs. Victor, the choir leader, announced that we were to begin practicing for the Easter Sunday Service.

Our first song was *Panis Angelicus*. I shall never forget the sense of warmth that filled my very being. Here I was on firm ground. A hymn I knew and loved. I think Ma must have sent this as a sign, as this was the same song I had sung at the orphanage my very first Sunday.

The organ began to play, and without a moment's hesitation, I started to sing. I didn't realize it then, but before the song was finished, Mother was the only other person singing with me.

When the organ stopped, Mrs. Victor turned to Mother. *Well,*

Elizabeth, you clearly have found an angel with a voice that comes from heaven.

Mother smiled. *We are blessed to have Margaret as our daughter.*

Mrs. Victor turned to me: *Welcome, Margaret. You will be a fine addition to our beloved choir. We believe sung prayer is the opportunity for all of us to open our hearts to Jesus and praise him with the gift that music is in our lives. As St. Augustine said, 'Singing is praying twice.'*

Mother took my hand and gave it a quick squeeze. As with my encounter with the Christmas orange, I found myself filled with a sense of both wonderment and what I now know must have been gratitude. I felt safe. I was being accepted, at least by these people. It was a first step, and Mother had prepared me well for the start of the journey.

The choir remains a lynchpin in my life. After Mrs. Victor stepped down, I became the Director, even though I was not quite fifteen. To this very day, I love the choir's humanity, to see the faces of each person devoting themselves to the same piece of music. I bask in the teamwork. It makes me feel optimistic about the world we live in. When we work as one, our voices come together as if to embrace other. From the very essence of who we are, we find a unified voice that erupts from the bottom of our hearts.

On Christmas morning when I turned ten, magic appeared beside our Christmas tree. A piano. I could not speak when I saw it. I touched the wood, the ivories. *Is it ours, Mother?*

Yes, a gift from Father to both of us.

I flew into his arms, crushing him with all the might and strength I could muster. He was not a man for much physical contact, but I do remember his returned hug. For a man who preferred not to be swayed by the emotions of the day, that was quite the accomplishment.

Starting that evening, Mother and I sang while I tried my best to pick up the tune on the keyboard. While I was somewhat successful, Mother would have none of this half-hearted attempt to master such a fine instrument.

Within weeks, Mother bundled me up, and we were off to my first formal piano lesson. We had to travel almost an hour over the hill to Warsaw, where a Mrs. Brown was to be my instructor. And she was quite the character. Her bohemian style was not at all what I was used to in our Sheldon circle.

Mrs. Brown wore no corsets—an unheard-of breach of fashion in those days—but rather a light blue caftan that looked like it had escaped from the pages of the *Arabian Nights*. She wore small glass flowers in her hair, which was a color of red that I had only seen on our Bantam rooster.

Her name didn't suit her as she was much too colorful to be called Brown. She explained the discrepancy as we finished my lesson one afternoon. *You see, Margaret, I am Hungarian, a proud citizen of the greatest empire in all the world. When I came to this country and ended up in Warsaw, no one could pronounce my name, Palinkas. They made it sound like your pancakes. And Mrs. Pancakes, I could never be. So, one day I looked at these pancakes and they looked brown and yellow, so I decided to be called Mrs. Brown. Mrs. Yellow would not be acceptable.*

So, besides the music, my lesson for you today is that you can change things you want to change. And no matter what people call you, you know who you really are. And she pointed to her heart and then her head as she continued, *for this is where Margaret comes from. This defines who she is.*

Mrs. Brown came from Budapest, where she had become a concert pianist. She was a firm believer that one must study the great classical works, so I was introduced to Beethoven, Bach, and Brahms, a challenge unlike any I'd had before. Though school work and singing came easily, playing the great masters took concentration and practice.

In that first year, I did all I could to make sure I devoted the time and energy needed to perfect the craft. Father loved to hear me practice—I think the German composers touched a chord in him that reminded him of his ancestral home, something he never talked about to me.

I studied with Mrs. Brown for a little over two years, and gradually, I began to master the harder pieces. Mrs. Brown liked to experiment with sound and interpretation. She told me that by touching these black and white piano keys we make sounds that people hear in any language. *Close your eyes, Margaret,* she told me: *Listen to the sounds. They should paint a kaleidoscope of colors in your mind. For the composer is like a great painter, no matter where you are, or where you were born, or what language you speak, you feel that he is communicating only to you. His music makes pictures in your mind. And they are your pictures alone to enjoy and savor.*

Mrs. Brown understood what music meant to me like no one else ever has.

I loved visiting her house. For one thing, nothing matched. Her furniture was all over-stuffed and well-worn around the edges. There were pictures everywhere, with backgrounds of locales that looked foreign and exciting. Although they were seared and faded with time, Mrs. Brown was at the front and center of every group. And that is where I placed her in my life.

She was utterly unlike anyone I had come in contact with. While the church choir gave me acceptance in the community, and my playing at home gave Mother and Father pleasure, it was that hour a week that taught me how to make my own spirits climb. I fell in love with the touch of the keyboard. I learned that from Mrs. Brown.

And I can remember the day it ended. It had been just over two years since the start of my lessons. Mother was waiting patiently in the parlor when Mrs. Brown, robes rustling, turned to her. With her arms waving to the skies, Mrs. Brown said: *Mrs. Meyer, Margaret, is gifted. A gifted child. We must remove her from this one-horse town where she will learn no more. We must allow her to explore and grow her talent.*

I studied with the great Edward MacDowell, the greatest of all-American composers and a brilliant performer. Margaret is about to learn to play his 'Second Piano Concerto in D Minor,' which is magnificent. He went crazy, and then with a shrug she added, but what else can you do when you are such a genius?

His wife, Marian, is opening her house in New Hampshire for artists and composers, young and old, to come and create. I will go this summer. Margaret must accompany me. It will not be expensive, and it will be good for her to meet and mingle with others with such talent and creative expression.

This was all said with great flourish and though I had never seen a live stage performance, I would have placed Mrs. Brown in the ranks of the great actresses. When she was finished, I was in shock. I held my breath.

Mother said not a word. She paid Mrs. Brown for my lesson and thanked her for her time.

There was no mention of New Hampshire, either on the ride home or ever again. It was the last piano lesson I ever took.

The piano is now in my house. I play it for and with my children. I play it alone. I play it with others. It is my friend and my support in good times and in bad. It holds my memories and inspires my dreams. Music is my life blood.

Belle

My memory of my first day at school revolves around a force that continues to make a difference in my life.

I was standing by myself in the playground feeling very much alone when this beautiful girl came up to me. She was tall with blonde hair that fell in ringlets softly around her face and eyes as green as the rolling hills that frame our countryside.

So, you are the new girl everyone is talking about, the one with the funny accent and the beautiful voice. My mother told me I should be nice to you because you sound like an angel when you sing. I think Mama wants me to get closer to angels so I will be less troublesome. I am not sure that is going to work, but we should be friends anyway.

My name is Belle George. They say I'm nothing but trouble. It's good to be friends with me because all the other kids will leave you alone. They know better than to mess with me.

She put her arm around me, and I knew from that moment on I would be safe. Rather than the Archangel Michael, I had my own protector, and she was Belle.

Her siblings were all brothers, five of them, so I became the little sister she never had. When I said something that wasn't quite right and the other kids began to twitter and put their heads down on the desk to keep from laughing, it was Belle who came to my side.

Early on, when a group of the girls were talking about the church picnic and the games that were to be played, I wanted to know more details so I asked: *What's the craic?*

One of the girls shrilled back: *Talk American, you Mick! We don't understand you. No wonder your father left you in an orphanage.*

My shoulders slumped, and I didn't think I could breathe. Out of nowhere, Belle appeared and knocked the girl down. She fell into the dirt, and Belle stood over her, fists pumping in the air as she looked around at the other girls who quickly ran away.

She looked down at the girl, who was still too shocked to sit up. *Your father would put you in an orphanage if he could because you're so stupid and ugly. You talk to my friend like that again, and you'll have to answer to me. So, get up and run home. And if you tell your Mama what just happened, I'll tell her that I was defending the voice of the angels. Then we'll see who gets a lickin'.*

From that day on, I was never teased directly again. That doesn't mean I ever felt really at home in those early days in the classroom. But as my accent faded and my stature as a soloist in the church choir became known, I became more and more accepted by the others. Still, my only friend in the entire town was Belle.

I was an outsider looking in, but when I was with her, Belle drew the circle and made me a part of it. We were quite the pair, as opposite in looks as two could ever be. Belle was tall and slender and though I was taller than most, I could never quite reach her in height though easily exceeded her in the span around our waistlines. Belle's features were as delicate as the lace in Mother's sewing basket while my mirror reflected freckled skin and a face that lets you know what I am thinking even before I start to speak.

By the time she was not quite fifteen, Belle left school, saying she had had enough of books. She took a job as an assistant in a fancy ladies' shop in East Aurora, and we would see each other in church on Sunday. I missed her from the day she left school and would count the days until she returned home. On those days, I would find my way to her house and we would fall into that easy chatter of best friends. I was involved in my school work and Belle was becoming more worldly wise but it simply didn't matter. There was a bond between the two of us that neither time nor distance would break.

Within a year, she moved to Buffalo and found a similar job at an exclusive dress salon, a major feat for one so young from such a small town. She was soon selling dresses to all the rich ladies who came in looking for the latest trends and fashions. She would come home most weekends to get a decent meal and fresh air. When she came to visit, she would regale us with stories that I could only imagine in my wildest dreams. She was becoming the "Belle of Buffalo."

Belle got prettier and prettier as the months wore on, blossoming with self-confidence.

I remember Mother being scandalized when Belle talked about corsets. *We don't speak of undergarments in this house, Miss Belle George,* Mother scolded.

Oh, but Mrs. Meyer, they have such wonderful names: La Fiancée and Swanbill. Women believe if the name is beautiful and the material lavish, physical beauty will be theirs and a husband will soon either be found or kept happy. I tell them how elegant they will look. How their figures will look just like mine. Belle howled and strutted around the yard. *Some of them are built like the cows in the barn and some like the chickens in the coop. But they want to believe that beauty and matrimony are theirs for merely $5.00 and a bit of pain and discomfort.*

Belle grimaced and preened around the garden as if she were one of the ladies in question. Even Mother laughed. Belle was the star, as bright as any in the constellation that showered us with its light each evening.

Teacher

Unlike Belle, for me, school was my favorite place to be. I never wanted to leave. However, it was my appointment as a teacher that caused quite a stir in this small town.

From day one at school, I moved quickly through my lessons. I loved to read, and there were not enough books to quench my appetite. Mother shared the passion, and we would often read to each other at night. Father was content just hearing our voices.

By the time I was fourteen, I had passed my peers in all subjects and began to help with teaching the youngsters, whose number seemed to be multiplying. I was given the title of "Senior Girl" and was happy in my role assisting the other children.

Mr. Altimeter, who had taught at the school for years and referred to himself as "Headmaster," clearly liked the arrangement. He could huff and puff about all the work he had to do, while I scurried around looking after the children in this one room school house, helping them with their lessons while still making sure there was enough coal to keep us warm.

Mr. Altimeter reminded me of Humpty Dumpty before the great fall. He was oval rather than round, and his body seemed to need another head to balance it. His family had immigrated from the North of England, a rare commodity in this town, and though he was Sheldon born and bred, he envisioned himself something of a country gentleman turned scholar. In all the years I worked with him, I never saw evidence of either.

He did, however, try to look the part. He would dress for school in a single-breasted Norfolk tweed jacket, with a half-belt that barely stretched over his ever-increasing waistline. He and Mrs. Altimeter had no children of their own, and he liked to say that he thought of every one of his students as his. He was not an unkind man, just a bit befuddled at times.

As the village's population grew, it was clear a more formal separation between the younger and older children in the classroom had to be arranged. Even with the older boys' sporadic attendance as they began to assume more and more responsibility for the farming chores, there simply was not enough room to keep the children seated and settled.

A small room in a nearby church was found and set aside as a classroom for the children from 6 to 8 years old. When Mr. Altimeter announced he would be looking for a teacher to help with that class, I asked why I could not take the position since it was essentially the role I was already performing.

Well, you would have thought that the devil incarnate had come to call. Mr. Altimeter turned crimson. His eyes narrowed, and he looked as if I were transforming into some formidable creature right before him. He sputtered something about my being a girl, and no woman had ever taught in Sheldon before. He wasn't about to break that tradition.

I had the good sense to keep my mouth shut, though I wanted to shout it was 1907, we were in the 20th Century, and someday women would be allowed to vote! I thanked him for his time and hoped he would reconsider his options.

He mumbled something unintelligible and returned to reading his book whose pages never seemed to turn.

That night, I spoke to Mother about the injustice of it all. To my surprise, she agreed. *We will not talk more about it tonight, Margaret. I expect you will go to school tomorrow and continue your duties as if the conversation has ended.*

I was baffled but had learned our discussion on the topic was indeed ended for the moment. I could fret and stew, but Mother would hear no more.

What happened next has never been quite clear. My guess is Mother somehow persuaded Father that it was his responsibility to help me secure the position of classroom teacher. To this day, I am not sure how she did it, for he was not particularly keen on my being perceived as a "working girl." The best I have been able to piece together was that the members of the School Board were canvassed. I imagine Mother had a chat with more than one of their wives. Whatever took place, Mr. Altimeter was convinced I was the best candidate for the position.

I can still see him behind the desk as he told me of "his" decision, one made in recognition of the good work I had done, my relationship with the children, and my standing in the church choir. He handed me the *Rules of My Engagement,* ending the conversation by acknowledging these were the same rules women teachers across the country were expected to follow and he was sure I would have no trouble following them as well.

I remember them to this day:

- I was not to marry during the term of my contract.
- I was not to keep company with men.
- I could not ride in a carriage with any man unless he was my father.
- I was not to smoke cigarettes.
- I was not to dress in bright colors.
- Under no circumstances was I to dye my hair.
- I must wear two petticoats.

- I must not wear a dress shorter than two inches above the ankle.

I didn't care about any of this. I was to be a teacher! I thought I would burst with joy.

I thanked him profusely, grabbed the aforementioned *Rules,* and literally ran home, my skirts flying and my hair breaking away from its tightly-rolled bun catching the wind in every direction. I could barely breathe by the time I opened the kitchen door and yelled out *Mother!*

She was in her garden, humming to the young seedlings as she gently pulled the weeds preventing them from taking over their chosen earth. The sun caught her newly acquired and ever-increasing gray hairs, making them glitter as if strands of silver were braided throughout her remaining jet-black tresses. She was just about to raise the watering can to quench the thirst of her new sprouts when I staggered into the scene, out-of-breath and arms flailing.

I shouted I was to be the teacher. *A teacher,* she nodded. *Well, now you must behave like one.* She smiled and told me to go comb my hair, as I was no longer a child. With that, she went back to her weeding and hoeing. Mother's *Rules of Engagement* were much more challenging to abide by than anything Mr. Altimeter could hand down.

I remember the thrill when the first child called me "Teacher," though I cannot remember what the question was or, even more sadly, who the child was. Happily, my years as the Senior Girl in school prepared me well for what to expect.

What I did not anticipate was that I was still responsible for my Senior Girl duties: bringing the firewood to light up the pot-bellied stove, and pumping the well water for drinking and hand washing for both classrooms. I recall summoning up all my courage to ask Mr. Altimeter if I were to be given someone to help me with the same chores I had performed these last three years. He merely smiled and told me if I didn't think I could handle the responsibilities of running my classroom, I might want to rethink whether or not I wanted the job. I was, after all, the first woman teacher that Sheldon ever had.

I cannot recall my response; I think I was too stunned to answer. Whatever the reply, he must have been satisfied. I remember being miffed. I was to do all I had done before plus prepare the lessons, score the exams, and teach the younger children.

When I went home, I told Mother about the conversation, saying I didn't think it was fair. I knew in my heart that if I were a male teacher, I would be treated differently. But Mother told me I must accept my situation in life and be grateful I got the job. She warned me if Father heard me complaining about Mr. Altimeter and my situation, he might forbid me to go back to the classroom. Father never quite understood my search to find my place in the world.

My head was shouting: *But I am a grown woman. I should be allowed to do what I want to do, and what I can do. I am a good teacher. Better than Mr. Altimeter on his best days!*

But I knew better. My ranting would only cause Mother to frown and wouldn't change the situation. I had learned my lessons well over the years. I simply accepted the situation and began to figure out what to do next.

Looking back over those days, I loved almost every minute. I was able to keep the classroom in order, making a game of gathering the firewood, bringing in the water, and rotating the seating in the winter so that the stove's warmth was equally shared.

In April of my first year, Mr. Altimeter asked me to stay after my class had been dismissed. He sat behind his desk, the ever-present opened book in hand. The conversation only lasted a few minutes.

After a bit of hemming and hawing, he straightened his tie, which wasn't the least bit crooked, and told me he was not displeased with my work this past year. He went on to say that if it were agreeable with my Father, I could continue in my role the next school year.

Remembering Mother's admonition, I thanked him for his kind words and said I would speak with Father and let him know of his decision by the end of the week. He told me I was a "good girl" and then went back to his reading, or at least pretended to.

I was both overjoyed and miffed. I was being asked to stay on. To teach. With the right mixture of chalk and challenge, I knew I was making a difference in the lives of my students. And I had to get Father's permission to continue doing what I knew was the right thing to do. Father would be fine. But it should be my decision alone.

I spoke with Mother first. We agreed Father should speak with Mr. Altimeter directly—that would make him feel that, as the headmaster, he had won, while still giving me what I wanted: another year as a teacher.

Belle Marries

Belle came home to tell us she was getting married to John, an engineer on the Erie Lackawanna Railroad. He was tall, with hair and eyes the color of the coal that kept the train engines stoked and running. His hands were strong and calloused; his face mostly without expression other than a lopsided grin that lit him up like a lantern the moment Belle entered the room. In both his physical presence and manner, he had a quiet strength. I knew Belle had met her match.

Belle asked me to be the witness for her marriage, an honor I was thrilled to accept and one that seemed only natural. Eli her older brother was to stand with John, who was an only child.

It was only after our first meeting with John that we learned that Belle had met a Prince Charming. As it turned out, he was not just a railroad engineer. Rather, his grandfather had been one of the original investors in the Western New York and Pennsylvania Railroad, and John was heir to the family fortune. He worked for the railroad simply because he liked trains.

All of Sheldon was shocked to learn Belle had landed a rich husband.

Belle contended she never knew her prospective groom had money until, after she had already agreed to marry him, he took her to meet his mother. When John pulled the carriage up to his house on Delaware Avenue, she thought he was playing a joke on her. As she walked up the imposing brick-lined stairway that shouted, "money lives here," she asked if his mother worked for the family. John's response was simple: *No, dear, we ARE the family.*

John's mother was one of Buffalo's grand dames, a role she devoted all of her time and energy to following the death of John's father over ten years ago. From the beginning, she disapproved of Belle; a shop girl from the farm was not who she had intended for her only son. But Belle loved John, and he clearly adored her. That seemed enough for both of them.

When it came time for the wedding plans, the debates surrounding the Missouri Compromise paled by comparison to the discussions of where the ceremony was to take place. In the end, it was decided the marriage be held in Buffalo with John's mother presiding over it all. While Belle's family was prominent in our small town, they were to be guests rather than players in the staging and execution of this event.

My first meeting with John's mother was at the tea she hosted at her home three days before the wedding. I thought it was a lovely gesture, a true invitation on her part to get to know Belle's family and friends. I was mistaken on all counts.

Upon my arrival, the most formidable creature I had ever seen made her way to meet me. I had never understood the word "haughty," but here it was personified. She came with her head high and had I not known better, I might have curtsied as she had all the trappings of someone who expected you to bow down and know your place. Her eyes were sharp and unkind. I had seen auctioneers appraise cattle with the same look she gave me. Immediately taking stock, she must have concluded that I was of no importance and would do little harm. She repeated my name slowly followed by: *You are the one that she chose to witness her marriage?*

When I replied *yes*, and started to say how happy I was for both Belle and John her eyebrows arched and with barely a nod, she turned her back. With a flourish of rustled silk, she went back to the safety of her own friends. Her cronies huddled together like a flock of crows chattering under the living room's immense crystal chandelier that illuminated carved mahogany walls into patterns of intricate designs and caveman-like shadows. The only warmth in the room generated from the embroidered silk shawls gracing the velveteen sofas—patches of bright flowers bringing a semblance of grace and delight to this staged prop of an inviting home. The women all wore the same style of clothing, spoke only to each other, and nodded in unison when an opinion was offered. For indeed, it was only their opinions that mattered.

To John's mother and her kind, what mattered was the labels on the china, crystal and silver tea services displayed on tables covered with white damask, not the integrity, manners and morals of the individuals in the room. I remember thinking the women in Mother's quilting parties were of better quality than any of the women I was laying my eyes on, despite their finery and uptown addresses.

One of the maids of the house was named Bridgit and had just come over from Ireland. Hearing her speak in a lilt I recognized only too well made my head turn. She sounded like so many that I had once known and I immediately wanted to make a connection. She returned my gaze, her eyes bright with hope, while hiding her hands red and raw behind the white starched apron that boldly claimed her status in life as a maid.

I started to approach, wanting only to hear her speak again, when Belle took my arm and pulled me away.

No, Margaret, Bridgit is a servant and you are not to chat with her like she is a friend. Someday we will all be treated as one. But this is John's mother's house, and as much as we don't like it, we need to play by her rules. She gave me a wink and a quick hug and whispered in my ear: *Someday it will be our rules. Then we will show everyone a thing or two.*

I walked away from Bridgit and felt those bright eyes bore a hole into my abruptly turned back.

I smiled weakly at Belle and followed as she ushered me to the largest and most beautiful piano I had ever seen. I quickly forgot my regret at deserting Bridgit as waves of pleasure engulfed me just to stare and marvel at this grand instrument. Belle and I agreed that I was to entertain the guests with a medley of current tunes.

The chatter in the room continued as I sat down at the bench and gently touched the keys. Every piano has its own essence, its own dignity. I paused, introducing myself through my nervous fingers, asking its permission to make music. As I lifted the cover, I saw my reflection in its ebony shine. A handsome face stared back at me, full of anticipation and expectation, though her hair showed a lack of discipline in keeping its braided bun in place. Not a beauty, but a young woman who understood the power of what can be accomplished when the instrument and the musician are intertwined. We were to become one, this piano and I. We understood and acknowledged the need we had for each other. It is an emotion hard to describe but a calmness overtook me. I was ready. So was the piano.

I smiled as I lifted my fingers and the notes responded to my touch. I had never felt so majestic and so comfortable at the same time. It was magical. I sang and played for almost an hour. The room became quiet, even John's mother stopped chatting. I noticed one or two of her friends tapping their toes to the music and knew that all was well.

Belle had been sitting alone next to the piano while I played. She had the look of a woman totally in control of the moment, knowing that the act we were performing was well-conceived and well-executed. She had not asked John's mother permission for me to play but assumed the role of the soon-to-be mistress of the house. I did not disappoint. When I played the current hit, *Any Old Place I Hang My Hat is Home*, Belle's eyes twinkled and her lips curved up. I actually had to stop myself from laughing out loud as I got the joke. It was a long way from the simple farmhouse on Buffalo Hill Road to this mansion on Delaware Avenue.

A couple of John's mother's friends extracted themselves from their tight corner to congratulate me on a fine performance. His mother squinted unkindly at the fuss being made, and I was glad for it. We may be from the farm, but God has given us talents. I slowly stood and lovingly touched the cover. The ivory keys that moments ago had delighted and entertained were once again quiet. I said a brief prayer and thanked this most beautiful instrument for the pleasure of its company.

It was clear, as I watched John and Belle in those days leading up to the wedding, that John was besotted with her. And she with him. Yet in the most surprising turn of events, Belle's brother Eli started to pay a great deal of attention to me. In all the hours I had spent at Belle's home as a child, neither Eli nor I had taken much notice of each other. But now he was at my side whenever I turned around. When one of John's train friends stepped up to meet me, Eli interrupted the introduction by asking if I needed my punch glass refilled. When I agreed, he took me by the elbow and led me away without so much as a 'nice meeting you' to the young man who come to meet me.

As the oldest brother, I always thought of him as quite formidable. Even then I knew though I liked the attention and thought he was nice enough, I was sure I would never look at him the same way Belle looked at John. But then, I doubted any man would ever look at me the way John looked at her, as if she were the only thing in the room worthy of his regard. While I believed that someday I might marry, it would be a different relationship than what Belle would have. I would be a partner, a working partner for certain. Belle, on the other hand, was a prize, to be worshipped and adored.

Their wedding was at St. Joseph's Cathedral and was presided over by the Bishop. Even Mrs. George was impressed. If she were not able to marry off her only daughter in her own parish, at least the Bishop would bless their vows.

The day of the wedding, I preceded the bride down the aisle. I looked quite lovely even though it sounds boastful. I had thinned out by then, my freckles had faded, and with Belle's help, my hair was under control. I would never be called a beauty as my features are strong, my skin prone to burn. The exception is my eyes. They are like no others, as they are neither blue nor green but a combination of both. They are the part of me that is the constant reminder of my Ma and Nell, for when I look in the mirror it is with their same eyes.

And it is that reflection in the mirror—the dark hair, fair skin and light eyes—that continues to look back at me and smile. For it is me; it is who I am and it will do.

Despite all the preparation and with Eli solemn and stalwart at my side, my insides were shaking. I had never had so many people looking at me. Then I realized they were not looking at me but waiting for Belle to appear. And finally, she did, on the arm of her father who looked like he couldn't wait to get back into his overalls and boots.

Belle was stunning. She came down the aisle as the peals from the Hook and Hastings Organ literally shook the rafters of the church. Her dress was of soft, rich cream-white satin, trimmed with lace. A wreath of orange blossoms held her veil. It seemed like we were in heaven and Belle, all pink and white, the head cherubim.

John, however, continued to defy his mother by foregoing the traditional morning dress in favor of the latest trend promoted by Belle. He wore a tuxedo. I had never seen anyone dressed like him before and thought he looked quite elegant and modern.

It was a strange match: Belle all ethereal and gauzy; John quite straight-laced in black and white. Maybe this is the contrast that is needed in a marriage.

When we got to the lowest step at the altar, Eli and I moved aside, leaving space for the bridal pair. John took Belle's hand and brought her forward, where they both knelt on an elaborate cushion. Then the Bishop blessed them and the marriage ceremony began.

When John went to place the ring on her finger, I thought he was going to pull off her entire glove. What did I know about such things? Her glove was made with a removable left ring-finger to facilitate easy access. Amazing.

After the ceremony, John and Belle marched down the aisle strewn with rose petals. A fairy princess and her Prince Charming, looking as if no one else was present.

The reception was back at John's family home. The servants passed platters of small bits to eat that Eli mistakenly thought was the dinner we were to consume. He was whispering in my ear his displeasure with the fare, when the ballroom doors opened and table upon table of food of every kind was spread before us. Spiced baked hams, crowded against salads of elaborate designs competed with turkeys roasted to a chestnut glow. All platters jockeying to find space at tables groaning with more food than I had ever seen at one time. Eli smiled, *now we're talking*, he chuckled as he took me by the arm and found our seats at the table. We danced, drank champagne, and toasted the new couple as they departed for the train to travel to New York City for their honeymoon.

It was in the midst of the party Eli asked if he could call on me when we got back home. I said "yes." Maybe it was the champagne, or maybe because I wanted to feel the same happiness I saw in Belle. He is a good man. And since I didn't see a rich railroad heir in my future, I thought, "Why not?" Mother would be happy and Father pleased.

While the memory of the wedding and Belle's happiness still fresh, such sadness broke the spell. In early June, less than a year after they were married, John was killed.

He was the engineer on a double-header freight train that

collided with a stopped train carrying twelve tons of dynamite. Four other people were killed and seven injured.

Eli went to Vestal, where the accident occurred, to bring home what was left of his body. The funeral was held here in Sheldon, and he is laid to rest in his family's plot in Buffalo. Belle was inconsolable. I could do nothing but hold her and let her cry.

John's mother was in Europe at the time. Belle sent a telegram to tell her what had happened. She never received a reply.

Through all this, Eli was a pillar of strength. It was then I made up my mind I would marry him, should he ask. No one else was showing much interest, and Mother's health was beginning to decline. She told me she would not be content until she saw me married, with a home of my own. She was praying she would one day hold my child in her arms. I decided I could do this for her.

I told Belle about my decision even before I understood it myself. It was about six weeks after John had died, and she had written she was coming home to say good-bye, she was leaving the country. We went for a walk in the woods near the pasture. Already slender, she had lost too much weight and her skin had become shallow, her eyes dull.

She said she had to leave Buffalo and even New York. Her loss was too great to bear, and she had to be around things that didn't remind her of John. He was everywhere she looked, she said, even in the air she breathed.

And the empty bed. I don't know how to sleep in an empty bed without the warmth of him beside me. I need the scent of his cologne on my sheets. His coffee cup in my sink. These are all gone from me now. And they will never come back. I lost him and our child within a month.

I gasped and took her hand in mine, I could find no words of comfort.

Oh yes, I was pregnant but so early not even John knew. The grief was too much and God took the last piece of John from me. It is too much right now. I need to forgive God for taking away my happiness.

I brushed away the tears falling from those green eyes that had once shone with such delight. Her shoulders slumped as she stood up to take her leave. I took her in my arms finding no words that might bring her comfort. As we walked silently to the door, she whispered in my ear, *I pray one day we will be true sisters.* She squeezed my hands and was gone.

A month later I received a note from her: *I am leaving next week for London on the Carpathia and will be living abroad for an indefinite period of time. John left me a wealthy woman, though I would trade every penny for just one more day at his side.*

I grieve for John each and every day, but I cannot bear the thought of wearing these widow weeds any longer. Life is hard enough without seeing anything but a black mantel of crepe over all.

John's mother takes solace in wearing such garments. I think —like Victoria the Queen—she will dress in deepest mourning until she is called to God's heaven, though in my less charitable moments I question whether she will end up on that side of the Lord when her time comes.

Not to fear, Margaret. I am not replenishing my wardrobe with the blues and pinks I so adore. No, my trunks are packed with purples and soft mauves, trimmed with cream rosettes. Still appropriate, and merely looking at them makes me feel more alive than I have felt these past months.

I will write when I am situated in London.

I am over-the-moon with the news that someday we may be true sisters. Eli will do well with you at his side. I love you both very much and look forward to holding the heir to the George name when I return.

Eli

Perhaps it was not surprising that Eli was interested in me. It was only matter of a time, now that I look back on it. I had spent so much time at the George house, he was comfortable being around me. I never thought he paid any attention to me; but when Belle left to go to the City, it must have left a gap in his life he hadn't anticipated.

When he first asked if he could call on me during the preparation for Belle's wedding, I was a bit surprised. But his attentions were not unwelcome. It was not as if I were turning away a flock of suitors. Between being a teacher and the director of the church choir, I believe I was a bit too much to take on for most of the farmers' sons. Or at least that is what I rationalized. My quick tongue and independent spirit may have also contributed to their shying away.

I was not quite 19 years old, and there were not too many more years before 'spinster' would be preceding my name, a fate neither Mother nor Father wanted for me. I wasn't actually thrilled about it either. With no brothers, if I weren't married, Father's farm would go to one of my male cousins, as women were not yet allowed to inherit property. I had long given up any idea of joining the convent, as I knew the vow of obedience was not an option. Marriage for me, and those like me, was the only path to follow.

When Eli asked Father's permission to court me, you would have thought the Pope himself had come to call, there was such rejoicing at the house.

He is a good man, Margaret. Eli and I are cut from the same cloth, even though most of those Georges think they are French rather than good, hearty Germans!

And Father smiled, such a rare occurrence that Mother's face lit up.

So, although the idea I was essentially getting more of the same didn't exactly set my heart aflame, it was comfortable. I knew what to expect. Nothing more. Nothing less.

And there was no hurry. As the oldest son, Eli would inherit the farm when his father stepped down or died. The courting would last over a year before we were officially engaged, and during that time, I could retain my position as teacher. It was an arrangement that suited everyone involved.

I think the term "salt of the earth" best describes Eli. He has a look common to men who have spent their days and nights tending livestock, even taking on some of the same physical traits. He is neither short nor tall, neither thin nor fat. In the summer, as the sun tans his skin, he becomes all of one color —skin, hair and eyes all the same brown. Nothing of contrast.

His sturdiness speaks to who he is: reliable, trustworthy and straightforward. It is his hands that bring me comfort. Strong and calloused, they reveal more about the man than any of his words. Those hands are seldom idle, and only in prayer are they clasped together. Yet, they can show tenderness to all living creatures. I have seen him stroke the newborn calf and administer healing salve to the aging mare with such gentleness and concern for their safety and well-being. When he takes my hand in his, I feel we are one.

For Eli is a man comfortable with himself and his world. Change comes slowly and is embraced reluctantly. Even when it came to our marriage.

Our courtship became yet one more pattern in his life. We would see each other on Sundays after church, and he would come back to our house for dinner. Mother would make quite the fuss over him, and Father would be content to have a fellow farmer to talk with. I would help in kitchen, to show off—as Mother put it—my "wifely skills." After dinner, I would play the piano and sing the latest popular tunes. Eli would occasionally join in, looking quite full of himself when he finished the tune in full voice.

He and I would then walk around the garden, always in plain of sight of Mother, who sat on the back porch. No worry about my reputation being tarnished! The sun would be finding its way into the western sky and the cows settled in for the night when we would say our goodbyes. Father would hitch up the wagon and drive him back to his farm, until next Sunday when we would repeat the day once again. In the winter, we simply left out the garden walk unless it was a particularly fine day.

At the end of the first year of this arrangement, John William George, Eli's father, announced he was moving in with his sister, Florence.

Eli's mother had died a few months before after a brief illness, and his father seemed to have lost the love of the land. In all honesty, Eli had gradually taken over all the farm chores and responsibilities, so there was very little change when the time came and John William moved to North Java, about 15 miles east.

Once all that transpired, I was expecting we would set a date to be married. And I was clearly not alone. Mother was chomping at the bit like a filly at the starting gate to get me married and start having babies. But no actual proposal of marriage was forthcoming.

I think Eli liked life as it was. He had his routine. He had his farm. He had his woman. He might want a wife but saw no need to have one at the moment. For the farm work, he had hired hands to help, and it would be years before any potential sons could fill their shoes.

This is all speculation on my part. Good girls didn't question the intentions of their best and only suitor. My guess is it was Father who brought the matter to a head, probably at Mother's urging.

Father had gone over to Eli's farm, ostensibly to look at a sick cow. Now, Eli had had sick cows before, so I don't know why this one needed such careful looking after. Over dinner that night, I inquired as to the state of health of said cow.

Should be up and about by month's end, was the response.

The following Sunday was a fine day in early March, and Eli and I decided to venture out for our weekly stroll. In typical Eli fashion, he took my hand, and reminded me of how long we had been keeping company.

It's going on over a year now, Margaret.

Almost two, I reminded him.

He continued, without pause, with what must have been his practiced speech, *Now that the farm is mine, it is time to take a proper wife. So, let's move on.*

I have talked with your father, and he is in agreement with our getting married, now that I can properly provide for you. We will serve each other well, Margaret. You can rest assured of that.

There was no talk of love. Of a life of happiness. A road to be travelled together.

But Eli was right as these past two years have shown. We are well enough suited, and he is a good man. Though not schooled, he does not dismiss my love of learning. He knows how to work the land. And before anything else, I was taught to be a farmer's wife; that was my future.

And he is Belle's brother. That alone made him the catch of the town, in my estimation.

In saying yes, I was giving up my teaching job as married women were not allowed in the classroom. We were to devote all of our time and energy to the care of our husbands. The classroom responsibilities would be a distraction. Sheer rubbish, but I knew it was a cause I could not win.

Mother, naturally, was thrilled. She had given me so much,

and I felt I owed her a wedding, the hope of grandchildren, and so much more.

We were married on June 10, 1912, and I became Margaret George, a farmer's wife. That was what I was raised to be though it has never been a perfect fit. I continue to miss teaching, of being in charge of something that brings a different challenge each and every day. I have had to give up something I wanted. For Eli, the farm and the land are all he ever wanted. And now his picture of what life should look like was complete.

I think I love Eli best during the harvest time, for that is when he is most happy. Autumn has men and boys moving from farm to farm, working, talking and sweating side-by-side. All with work to be done and a sense of accomplishment when the day has ended. And Eli relishes being a part of it all. From fields of hay lighting the countryside in flickering shades of gold come lusterless yellow bundles of straw and grain that are our lifeblood during the cold days and long nights to follow. It is Eli's job to provide for all who depend upon him, a job he was born into. The job that defines him as a man.

I recall a midsummer's day when we first married. Eli found me in the garden. The spring flowers tended by his mother were gone and I was puzzling about how I was going make this patch of dirt my own. He knelt down beside me and took the soil in his hands. *This is our land, Margaret. You will find a way to make these flowers bloom in your own way.* And he kissed me gently on the cheek and took the dirt from his hands and gently placed it in mine. I remember feeling loved at that moment.

For Eli is one with the land, it defines him and gives him

purpose. I have always needed more, even when I can't define what more means.

Motherhood

I grew up on the farm and watched animals mate from the time I was old enough to comprehend what was going on. Sex is a natural and needed part of farm life, and there are no romantic illusions about it.

And so, it is in my married life. Eli is kind in the marriage bed, but like the good farmer he is, he has a routine and schedule to be followed. I am to perform my "wifely duty," as Mother so subtly phrased it, whenever he needs to be satisfied.

He reaches for me, nuzzles my neck, and is quickly on top. Grasping my shoulders, he finds his way into me. After a few short minutes, he rolls away. He is satisfied, the deed having been done. It is not unpleasant, and, at times, I wish there could be more. More exploration, more touching. More about me and less about him.

But it is a quick squeeze, a *Good night, my dear*, and a quick kiss on the lips. Then we are done for the night. And this labor has borne such fruit. I am already a mother, one of the most exciting and exhausting roles there is to play.

When I first announced I was pregnant, Eli burst with pride. We had been married but four months, a record for even the best of the young farmers in the area. My first child. The thought stunned me into silence. I had a baby growing inside of me. Amazing.

Mother couldn't contain herself. This was the moment she had been waiting for—to have and hold a grandchild.

The next few months were all about me and the baby. Eli looked at me in awe as my belly grew bigger and the baby's movements could be mapped on my ever-expanding frame. He somehow seemed taller, taking on the role of family protector. My feelings for him grew in a way I had not yet imagined, a deepening sense of commitment to our way of life, our farm, and our soon-to-be family.

Mother was sewing and knitting up a storm. Whatever the sex, this baby was to be clothed and swaddled in keeping with the true gift we were about to receive.

I had helped our local midwife in the past, so as the months wore on, I knew what to expect. However, it is one thing to observe, and quite another to play the leading role in this drama of life.

I woke up at about three on a hot and rainy early July morning with the disquieting sense that my waters were beginning to break. I wandered about the house for an hour or so, feeling some relief the waiting might be over. But that relief was dwarfed by terror of what was to come. Unable to sleep, I nonetheless went back to bed. Eli slept unperturbed by all the getting up and moving around.

Had I just felt a contraction? I lay in bed waiting in the darkness for another stab of pain. Sure enough, about ten minutes later a lightning bolt shot across my lower abdomen.

Eli, wake up! I'm in labor!

He moaned and rolled over. I shook him again, but harder this time.

Wake up! I hollered.

This time it worked, and he sat up, wiping the sleep from his eyes.

Are you sure?

I clearly knew what was happening. I had never felt pain like this before in my life. *I need Mother,* I howled.

He went out to the barn and sent one of the workers to get Mother. When he arrived back at the bedside, he looked terrified.

Go, I said. *You are of no use here.*

It was all he needed to hear, and off he went.

Soon, Mother, the midwife, and her two daughters were at my bedside. I seemed to go in and out of consciousness. As the morning wore on, I became completely and mindlessly terrified. I shook, and I couldn't let go of the midwife's hand.

What are you afraid of, my love?

I didn't know how to respond to this. I was 23 years old, what was I afraid of? Dying? More pain? Producing a stillborn or deformed baby? I was afraid of every trauma and terror that has dogged this life-threatening process of giving birth.

The sun was high in the heavens when I thought the end was in sight. Everything about giving birth had taken longer than I expected. I pushed for an hour and a half. Finally, my child decided to make an appearance.

In great excitement the midwife said, *Give me your hand.*

She took my hand and placed it on the top of my baby's head, as it was emerging. I have never before or since known such a magnificent moment. I still can feel that soft, alien skin, the fuzzy top of a rubbery boned head, the sense of wondrous, unknowable new life. In two more pushes my son was born, and I heard him cry.

Leon John was by far the most beautiful baby I had ever seen. I didn't sleep that night, tired as I was. I stared at the little creature swaddled tight in his blanket and wondered whatever I was supposed to do now. Fortunately, from that moment on, he began to tell me. My whole life had changed forever.

I now wonder how my own Ma felt the first time she held me in her arms.

My Daughter

It was only 13 months later that Louise was born. She came so easily that I was wide awake and feeling fine following her birth. Eli had cooed over his 'little girl' and found me later that day staring at her as she quickly found my breast and proceeded to take her fill.

A daughter, I have a daughter. A prayer rose in my heart, disbelief flooding me as I looked at all her perfect parts. Her nose, the fine threads of such dark hair curling around the curve of her ear. I could only thank God for this most precious gift.

Leon wasn't sure what to make of all the fuss. That evening, he found me lying on the bed nestling the newborn in my arms. He reached out his hands to his baby sister as Eli came into the room. Eli knelt down to give him a closer introduction, and Louise attached her small hand to his finger as he smiled at this precious child. This was a family. I felt a pang in my heart so deep it overwhelmed me.

Mother was ecstatic for now she had a baby girl to teach and love. The years, however, were taking their toll on her. She seemed to be getting shorter, her eyes more distant. She and Father would be found sitting in their chairs by the fire even on warm evenings. But the new baby, a girl; this was a gift for her to cherish. It gave me joy to see her so happy, even though it was for such a short period of time.

Belle Returns

After Eli and I were married, Belle sent me a silver brush and mirror as my wedding gift. There was a note telling me I was to look closely in it each evening to remind myself how beautiful I am, each and every day. And it is that mirror that shows me the first strands of gray interweaving throughout my still dark hair and the fine lines that have begun to find a permanent home around my eyes and lips.

In the months and years to follow, I heard from Belle as she traveled the world. I prayed for her daily.

Belle was also the reason for the first fight Eli and I ever had. Imagine. His very own sister.

I had just received the most astonishing letter from her. She was still in London and had become friends with two fellow Americans, a brother and sister named Gertrude and Leo Stein. Leo, the brother, was an Art Collector, and Belle was introduced to him by one of her friends who was staying at the Savoy, the same hotel where she had been residing.

She wrote that his sister was like no one she had ever met before.

Gertrude has deep black eyes and clearly knows her own mind. I found her intimidating and appealing at the same time. Leo is a nice enough chap. They are moving to Paris soon. Leo extended an invitation for me to visit should I find myself on "the continent."

For now, I am content in London. But Paris…think of it, Margaret. The Eiffel Tower, the Seine—all the things I never studied in school, I could learn about first-hand. Maybe next spring.

Well, when I told Eli about Belle's meeting the Steins in London, he got angry. I have never seen him like this. He kept shouting that the Steins were Jewish, and Belle was Catholic and she should not be friends with such heathens. I told him Belle was a grown woman with a mind of her own, but that just made him angrier.

She needs a husband to control her.

I was stunned. *Control her?* I shouted. *Is that what you think you do to me? Control me? I am your wife, and the mother of your children, but you don't control me! If that is what you think you do, Eli George, you have another think coming!*

I stormed out of the kitchen. We didn't speak another word. That night, I pretended to be asleep when he came to bed, still too upset to have him roll over on me.

The next day the sun rose as usual. Eli was about his business as if the conversation had never happened. I fretted and stewed a bit longer but no more was said. For Eli that was yesterday's conversation, it has nothing to do with today or tomorrow.

Belle went on to Paris later that spring and took up the Steins' invitation to call on them. She said it was a "soiree," but it simply sounded like a church gathering to me. Lots of people talking about things that interest them. In Sheldon, we talk about children, crops and chickens. In Paris, they talk about art and books.

Then, more than four years after the day she left, Belle came home. I was filled with mixed emotions when I got the telegram. During the months she had been gone, she had seen the world. I was part of the world she left behind, a wife and mother portraying the same roles as our mothers before us.

I was in the kitchen preparing lunch when Belle opened the kitchen door. I gasped out loud when this stylish woman in a tweed suit and crisp white blouse came into view. Her hobbled skirt tapered to reveal slender ankles encased by the most exquisite pair of black patent leather boots, with a square buckle in the front. And the hat: all velvet and ostrich feathers, shading those green eyes that had now seen so much of the world.

She looked taller, and more beautiful, then I remembered, her youthful good looks now having been replaced by sophistication and worldliness, touched with the shadow of sadness.

I was in my everyday house dress, apron tied at the waist,

with Leon playing with the pans at my feet and his sister in the cradle by the fire.

I gasped, *I didn't expect you so soon!*

I wanted to see you as soon as I arrived. I have missed you so, my sister was her reply.

With that, she fell into my arms so heavily that her hat fell off. Once all was gathered, she pulled out of her bag, the most beautiful china tea pot. White porcelain with delicate pink roses hand-painted, it looked like a slice of my garden was being cradled in my hands. *I have traveled many a mile protecting this pot as if it were it made of gold to bring to you,* she laughed. *My diamonds and pearls were not nearly as guarded. So, let us have it steep my homecoming cup of tea and then it will be time to break into Eli's cider.*

No way I am tarnishing this lovely piece with those brown tea leaves, I retorted, eyes smiling. *It is going on the highest shelf, so no little hands will think it a plaything to be toyed with.* And that is where it sits today.

Time evaporated. We laughed and talked the day and night away. Eli came in at what point and gave her a quick kiss on the cheek. *Good to have you back where you belong,* he told her. *Glad to be here,* was her response, *though I am not quite sure where I truly belong anymore.*

Well, this is where it is. He told her in the same tone he must have used to scold her as a child. Belle just smiled and said nothing. Nor did I. It is wonderful to have her close again. She has bought a house in Buffalo and has become quite involved in the political movement working to get women the right to vote. She wants me to get involved, but I keep telling her I have a husband, a farm, and two children. When I balked, in typical Belle fashion she responded: *And no vote.*

Mother and Father

And with the wonder of new life all around me and my joy in Belle's return, death knocked on my door. Loudly. Abruptly.

Mother died unexpectedly; she who had never been sick a day in her life. Father found her in her garden. A man of precision and routine, he had come back to the house for lunch, at the same time he always appeared. Mother was not there, and he knew immediately something was wrong.

He found her lying among her flowers, at peace and at rest.

I was lost. But it was Father who suffered the most. He became bewildered and confused. Without her, he had lost his sense of direction and purpose. We were in the process of selling the farm and making plans for him to move in with us, when he gave up on life and quietly went to join her. He died in his sleep.

I had lost both of them within two months, an overwhelming loss, but I have had little time to grieve. I needed to move on, to keep my family bathed, clothed and fed. It was the least I could do for both of them. To give to others the love and support they had given me all those many years.

A Farmer's Wife

Eli and I work well together with the farm as our focus for it is about the land, the children, the neighbors. All that is tangible. Early last year, he was open to my suggestion that I begin to keep track of the animals and their production. *It is not unlike what I did as a schoolteacher,* I explained. *I simply wrote down the test scores for each child, the books each had read, what plans I thought should be put in place for their next lesson.* He nodded, seeing the logic of what I described. He shares the information with me: how the hens are laying, what cow is producing, what fields are the most fertile. Already we are seeing a pattern of what is working is well, and he is making decisions based on the trends the ledger describes. *We make a good team, Margaret,* he said one night as we were looking at the numbers. *True partners as well as parents. You are a fine wife and I am a lucky man to have you.*

This was high praise from him, to recognize what I can contribute to the farm in ways other than bearing children, keeping the house, and selling eggs in the market.

But his life and his destiny are all very clear to him. I know in my heart my wanting to reach out and connect with my brother, is not something Eli would understand; his past and his present are so intertwined that he can see no difference. And there is little that is different than the life he has always known

Writing to James is something I know I must do. I ache with a nagging, unrelenting sense of loss. Burying Mother and Father opened an old wound, one that never truly healed from Ma's death and Da's abandonment. I don't know what it is like to be Irish, to have a heritage that is different than all that surrounds me. I feel a need to understand the part of me I lost in order to better understand and cherish the family that is now mine. I need to feel whole.

THE JOURNAL

I am not sure this is all there is about me, but it is enough. 1915 will be the year that I begin. It started with finding Mrs. Quinn's letter and now I will move from my past to my present. I already feel the healing and magic that comes from putting these words on paper. I make a solemn vow I shall continue to write in it as often as I can and as I need.

I will write to James tomorrow. At the moment, I don't intend to let Eli know about my plans. I am not sure he would understand, and I am not sure I could even explain why I am hoping to find my brother.

April

I started to tremble when I saw the return address on the envelope:

James Clancy, Dublin, Ireland

I had mailed my letter to him with a mixture of hope and

trepidation. I wasn't sure whether James or anyone who might know him was still at the address that I was given so long ago. Was he still alive? Would he even care to contact a sister gone so long that she might be considered dead? I worried that if the grave is where he placed her, that is where he might want her to stay.

I quietly placed the envelope in my apron pocket, like a small child hiding a treat to be savored in secret at another time. I worked feverishly to get the daily chores done, all the time the unread letter burning a hole in my pocket like the ember of a smoldering fire.

Hours later, the children were napping and Eli resting from the early morning planting when I grabbed the letter and fled to the garden. There among the trees that offered me respite from the mid-afternoon sun, I found a spot that offered me the solitude I craved. With a racing heart, I read:

My Dear Margaret,

I write with such joy I fear you will not be able to decipher my handwriting. I have thought about you and our wee sister often. A Mrs. Quinn had written to our Aunt Hannah to tell her our Mother had died on your voyage to America. Months later a letter arrived from our Da saying he had put you and Nell in an orphanage and he was heading west to find work. We never heard from him again.

Aunt Hannah was distraught and quite inconsolable for months. Had our Da given more information as to where you and Nell had been left, she would have sent for you.

She grieved not only for her beloved sister, but for the family now torn apart.

Our Uncle Andrew was a very successful banker, rising to the role of a Director at the National Bank of Ireland. There are not many of the Catholic faith in this kingdom who can claim that honor. Our aunt was renowned for her gift of voice and was happiest when there was a crowd of people gathered around her piano. She could entertain the whole evening long.

I am sad to share the news that they are both gone now; they died within a year of each other. That was very hard on me as I miss them both dearly. I do believe neither one would be happy living without the other, so perhaps it was for the best. May their souls rest in peace. They were very good people who loved and cared for me as if I were their own flesh.

Thanks to our uncle, I am employed by the same Bank and equally successful. I was educated by the Jesuits at University College here in Dublin, so am quite prepared to deal both with British bankers and Irish scoundrels—the likes of whom you often can scarcely tell apart. I married a lovely woman, Annie Mooney, and we have been happily wed for almost 8 years.

Unlike you with a growing crew, we have but one son, Jimmy. Annie was not as blessed with being able to carry and deliver new bairns and we lost three: one in her arms only minutes after giving birth and two who left us while still in her womb. Annie is a bit of a thing—our Ma would have called her a sprite—and her health has suffered badly from all these sad events. Jimmy was a true miracle for us.

He is but five years old, and a good lad who brings us much joy each and every day.

I remember you as a toddler with your long dark hair—often quite unruly—that framed such rosy cheeks and porcelain skin. You were always talking, and our Ma would call you her little magpie. From then, we just called you Maggie. So, with your permission, that is how I will refer to you in my letters. I will continue to pray our little sister Nell has found happiness. I know of no way to find her.

Aunt Hannah said I favor our Da in looks. So, if it helps your memory, I am closing in on six feet in height. I have translated the meters into feet to help you frame a better picture. In my younger days I was called strapping. However, the years and my fondness for Guinness and our cook's good skills have encouraged my waist to spread. Some may say my girth speaks of prosperity. I find it a bit too portly for the likes of me. That being said, there is little I do to make it go away, as the thought of shaking my head at a good meal or not sharing a pint or two with the lads dispels any hope of me returning to the fitness of my youth. My hair, thick and streaked with white, crowns my true banker's look. The mirror reflects the image of a conservative banker: a font of cautious monetary advice and wise financial counseling. Sometimes it is more the packaging than the contents that the customer is looking for upon first introduction.

I hope this finds you, your husband, and your children in good health. Please write often. I feel I have found a treasure that once was lost.

With love and affection from your brother,

James

Embraced by summer sun's rays, and the words I had just read, my body felt warm all *My brother*. How wonderful to say that phrase and know somewhere, someone remembers me as I was and loves me for the simple reason that we are family.

I know I have to wait before I tell Eli. He has never been comfortable with the fact I was born in Ireland. I overheard him telling the census taker two years ago that I had been born in New York. When I asked him why he hadn't said that I had been born in Ireland, Eli shook his head. *Who cares about that, Margaret? It was too long ago to matter, and besides you belong here now. You were raised by a German family, and if that is good enough for me and our children, it is good enough for you. It is tomfoolery to think of yourself as being anything else.*

I don't want to sound too excited about what I have found and what I intend to do, so tonight will not be the time. For the moment, I am giddy with the joy and hope of it all.

When I finally mustered the courage to tell Eli about finding my brother, he was less than pleased. *Brother? You have no brother, Margaret. You call Belle your sister, and even that is a stretch.*

The children were asleep and we were sitting at the table, so I tried to maintain a calm tone as I explained about finding the satchel and the letter. When I started to describe how wonderful it was to find the missing pieces of my life, Eli slammed his fist on the table. *I am telling you Margaret, this is sheer foolishness. You are American—not Irish. Who is going to start knocking at our door—a bunch of Micks who drink too much, can't read or write, and brag that we are relations?*

I was stunned. I have never heard him speak of any man in such a way as he spoke of the Irish. Shaking, both inside and out, I explained that James was a prominent banker in Dublin, educated by the priests of the Church, and there is no intention of sending any relatives—even if we had them—to New York.

He yielded some, but the scowl on his face was unrelenting. Then the conversation was dropped, as if it had never occurred.

I won't hide James' letters, nor will I make a great display when they arrive. I will continue to put the envelope in my pocket with its precious contents, to be read and reread when time allows.

What hurts the most is Eli does not nor will not see how important this is to me. He is surrounded by all he has known for his entire life. And he has always been clear about who he is and what he is to do. There are no questions to be answered in his world. He has followed a straight path.

That is not true for me. A piece of me is Irish, a piece that was left behind. Now I have the opportunity, if not to capture it, to at least recognize that which is mine.

Eli wants me to be his vision of me, even if it is not true. I need to be all I am capable of being.

May

I find I am once again a student after all these years. Someone, surely Belle, enrolled me in the Suffrage Training School, a mail-order course that outlines the issues and the need for women to get the vote. The first installment came today. My initial reaction was that I don't have time for all this nonsense. There are not enough hours in the day to finish what I need to do around the house and farm, let alone take time to complete a series of twelve lessons.

But I was intrigued and started to read the first set of materials. Now, I must admit, I am quite engaged. I realize how little I know about the history and the issues facing the movement.

We are women of the 20th Century and have a broader responsibility in the world. We need to care about the health and safety of our families: the food they eat, the water they drink, the diseases they may catch. We need to open our eyes to see what is happening in the world around us. We need to open our minds to understand what options we have under our control.

Our voices should be heard so that we can usher in a world of peace, not one of the petty strife and monarchial despots who are ravaging Europe today.

I am not sure that, even after graduating from Suffrage Training, I will call myself a "Suffragette." It seems a radical title for the likes of me. But I now want to be able to vote. I want my daughter to be able to chart a course of her own choosing.

I wrote to James about my initial awakenings and my concern about putting myself forward as an advocate for these changes. His latest letter was most encouraging, urging me to get involved. He understands, in a way that Eli and the men in this country cannot, that voting is not just a privilege but the right to have your voice be heard. It is something that all men and women must have to be truly free.

I am now involved.

Belle has the most amazing group of women friends. My head actually hurts having spent an evening with them. So many ideas. So much conversation. So much energy.

It was Belle's birthday, and Eli agreed I could spend the night with her in Buffalo. When I arrived that afternoon, she was flushed with excitement. Breathlessly, she told me that Carrie Lane Chapman Catt was coming to her soiree this evening. (What I would call a good old-fashioned gathering of neighbors, Belle labels "soiree," a leftover from her evenings with the Steins all those years ago.)

I was able to fill in the pieces, that this Carrie Lane is internationally known in the women's rights movement. Like Belle, she left for Europe after the death of her husband, and it was there she became engaged in the cause. She was an early president of the National American Woman Suffrage Association and is slated to return to that role next year.

I picked up on Belle's excitement and was not disappointed with meeting Mrs. Catt in the least. She captured the room, not by her presence, for she is neither plump nor lean and bony. Rather, she is quite ordinary looking, but with a strong voice and a clear mind. Her intelligent dark brown eyes were alight when she began to talk to us. And talk she did. Not down to us. Not at us.

With fervor, she told us we must incorporate the prospects of America entering the war in Europe into our work to secure the vote; she offered us what she called "The Winning Plan." Her words and passion inspired us.

As our world fights for democracy, we must continue to fight to have a voice in our government. Voting for women's suffrage is part of the struggle toward democracy in all corners of the world.

I lost my fear and became actively engaged in the discussion. The ever-present question: *What can we do?* Carrie Lane answered this as she mapped out her strategy. To pass the amendment in New York, we had to get the vote out, we had to be heard, we had to go house-to-house and tell our story. That was the lesson we learned from the amendment's failure in 1915.

To succeed today, we have to compel men to sign a petition stating that we want the vote. We have to climb tenement stairs, walk country lanes, and visit the homes of the rich and the poor. We must reach out to our sisters in our villages and in our cities and engage them in the discussion. We must have our voices heard.

She ended with the question: *Will you raise your voice with me?*

I couldn't believe I was the first on my feet to shout, *YES!*

All the others joined in, and soon we were laughing and hugging each other. Sisters united in a cause. And somehow, I have been transformed into a Suffragette, although one of my own definition.

We spent the rest of the evening devising our overall strategy.

I was to talk with the farmers' wives and come to Buffalo to help as needed. I could barely sleep that night, I was so excited. We meet again next week to finalize our plan of attack. I wonder if this is how Jefferson and Adams felt when they signed the Declaration of Independence: an irrevocable step when, in reality, there was no choice. You simply have to demand your right to be recognized and be heard.

I felt younger than I have in years.

When I came home and told Eli what I was going to do, his face turned red, and he slammed his fist on the table shaking the plates set for the evening meal. *You are a farmer's wife and a mother, not some radical woman marching up and down in front of the White House. Your place is in the home with your family, not gallivanting all over making a fuss!*

I had learned well enough from my evening at Belle's not to get angry or appear hurt. I simply asked him if he didn't want Louise to have the same voice and opportunities as Leon. He stumbled, unable to respond as I went on.

My role is to simply ask our friends and neighbors if they want women to have a voice, to have them help make the world safe for democracy. It is a simple question. If they say yes, they sign the petition requesting that women be given the right to vote in this state. If they do not, they don't sign it. I don't see how that can be a problem for anyone. And I anticipate you will vote yes when the time comes so that I have the same rights as you, Eli George.

He looked at me as if he were actually seeing me for the first time. His eyes widened and his hand slammed the table once again. *What in God's name is this world coming to?* he hissed. *Neither my mother nor Mrs. Meyer would ever have given a hoot as to whether or not they could vote. They saw their role as wife and mother as important enough for them. All of this talk about giving women the right to vote comes from those spoiled city women who don't have enough to do to keep themselves busy.*

Well, do what you want Margaret, but you have real responsibilities around this house that have to be met. And I expect you to continue to do so.

Seconds later, he headed for the barn without ever looking back. What does he think I am going to do? Forget about my family and my obligations to them? I love my children, but I need more in my life, to call it my life.

My path continues to be clear. I have my own mind. Both when it has to do with James and with my efforts to gain my right to vote.

July

Such a day. We were back at Belle's, finalizing our tactics to get petition signatures to resubmit the proposed amendment. As we laid out our plans to educate our neighbors about our cause, tempers began to rise. Although we all had the same goal in mind, it became clear very early that the paths to achieve success were diverging, to say the least. I stayed quiet as long as I could.

But hearing the city women speak of my neighbors and farm women with such a lack of respect caused my temper to flare. I don't know what words triggered the reaction, but I finally raised my voice—in the same school teacher tone I use to chastise the children when they are out-of-control.

Different people have different ideas about what they are willing to do to make themselves heard. I want to be clear: we cannot win this election without the vote of our farmers.

I have neighbors, good men and women, who argue that if women are given the vote, we will be giving up our roles as mothers and as partners in the daily workings of the farm.

Most of us—no, none of us—have the leisure time to spend talking about what we should do. We are too busy feeding our families, tending our crops, and harvesting our fields for such idle chatter. We are not going to sit at a meeting to hear someone talk down to us and tell us what we must do. Farmers' wives rarely have time to sit. And our home obligations are very clear each and every day.

For our amendment to pass, we have to make our arguments one-on-one. That is how it is in the country—we talk with our neighbors, and we listen to them.

You are sitting here blathering away in a vacuum about a world you know nothing about. These are not ignorant people who need to be shown the way. The only sheep we have are those that graze the land. These are hard-working people who need to understand why the change is important before they can accept it. Your preaching to them with your noses up and your spines unbending is not going to get them to come around to our way of thinking.

I paused, took a deep breath, and looked around. Belle's apartment, like her, was sophisticated, and a bit out-of-place for Western New York. Mirrors in geometric shapes and patterns hung on walls painted in shades of dark rose, jade green. There was silver leafing in her ceiling. Pillows in bright patterns and animal skins are tossed helter-skelter on the divans and chairs, making them look more fashionable than comfortable. This is a stark contrast to me who always looks more comfortable than fashionable, particularly since I am pregnant again.

I didn't belong in this world of glamour. Eli's admonishment: *You are a farmer's wife* reverberated in my head as I looked around this room that shouted color and exuberance. All I could hear was an unexpected and unwelcomed silence. The chatter and twittering ceased. Here I was, new to the cause, having the audacity to take them on.

The quiet seemed to last forever, though it was only seconds until Belle threw her head back, curls bouncing and laughed: *You tell us, Margaret. Farm women have been around cattle long enough that they can spot bull from a hundred feet away!*

She looked a bit sheepish herself when she added: *It's time I remember that.*

One of the other women piped in, not necessarily in a pleasant voice: *So, Margaret. What would you have us do?*

There I was with no real plan in mind. I smiled, looked at my unsmiling questioner and started to do what I have always done—engage my brain and start to talk.

We need to reach out into the communities with the message that rings true to them and their concerns. Letting our farmers know that giving women the right to vote protects the home, the family, the farm. This is not about jazz-age women marching in the streets of New York City or protesting in front of the White House. This is about preserving the integrity of the farm family. We believe in honest government and want our say to ensure it protects us, our children, and our land.

That is the message we need to share.

And let us tell the women what they can improve through the ballot box: better roads, better schools and libraries, and better use of taxes to help the farmer. It's not just about having our say; it is about making a difference.

My voice was breaking. *I know what I want. I want my daughter and her daughters to have more opportunities, more choices. I want my sons to respect women for their minds and listen to their opinions.*

With the vote, we can accomplish so much.

That is what we need to say. And we need to say it to them at their gatherings—lawn fetes, grange meetings, county fairs. Wherever they go, we must be there. And our message should be consistent and clear, no matter who is giving it.

And then I ran out of steam. I took a deep breath and sat down.

There was a nodding among most and then a sane voice was heard: *Margaret is right. Let's stop talking and come up with a more detailed action plan on how we are going to reach out to more people. Time is wasting. Let's get moving.*

And we did. We targeted churches, schools, the county fairs, church socials. Toward the end of the evening, Mary Macaulay, one of the pillars of the suffrage movement from its earliest days with Susan B. Anthony, offered to travel around Western New York, holding open-air meetings, bringing the public's attention to the cause.

I grew up on the land. I can speak to our sisters as one of them.

As I was leaving, Belle gave me a hug and, for my ears only, whispered: *You continue to amaze me, my sister. Gumption and a voice that needs to be heard beyond the church choir. You have come a long way from the little girl with the lilt in her voice that I had to defend in the school play yard.*

I felt more energized than I had in some time: my brain had not died, as I sometimes feared.

When I came home tonight, I took the pins from my hair and, holding the silver mirror given to me by Belle all those years ago, saw something in my eyes that I had not seen in too many years: self-confidence and determination. The young school teacher was smiling back at me, now a grown woman who can stand alone, not in the shadow of anyone or anything. I welcomed her back into my life.

Tomorrow I will find myself, once again, sweltering above a simmering hot stove stirring the berries for the preserves and jams that must be put up before the summer suns fade. But today I tasted something equally sweet—a hint of freedom that comes with being my own woman. Not a mother, nor a wife, nor a farmer. But Margaret, with an opinion and mind of my own.

It is a moment to savor.

January

Another baby girl. Florence came into our lives as the New Year dawned. Bald, blue-eyed with a pink gurgling sound, it was love at first sight. I believe she is the harbinger of good things to come, as I think she is mine alone.

Eli showed little excitement at the addition of another daughter. He has Louise, now toddling who responds to the sound of his voice with shrieks of joy.

February

There is talk of peace at any price in this country, and the war waging in Europe seems more than a world away. It is only the letters from James that bring the reality of such heartache home.

I can see both sides of the issue from the American perspective. I am not sure whether I side with those who shout that America must remain neutral or those who opine about our need to stop terrorism in Europe. I do know I am thankful that Leon is so young that there is no fear of losing him to the army. I am not sure I could survive the loss of any of my children to a cause so distant from us. Yet my heart was breaking as I read James's words.

> My Dear Maggie,
>
> The headlines in our newspapers shout of war and discord. On the streets of Ireland, our fighting for our land is commonplace. It is not just a dream or a desire. It is our fundamental right to govern ourselves. Unfortunately, the talk and hope for our country's independence is now set aside until all of this is settled. It is but one more disappointment on our road to Home Rule.
>
> The risk to the freedom of small nations such as Belgium or Serbia if invaded by a military aggressor is shared by

Ireland as well. To secure our freedom, we must be free from all foreign oppressors, not just the British.

With the war on our doorstep, our boys are signing up, I think for many reasons. Some because they perceive it as a just cause that must be won. Some because of the romantic notion of war—get a gun, see new countries, and return home a hero. Others because there is so little opportunity for them to succeed in the country of their birth. This is the saddest reason of all, for it is merely a form of economic conscription. Ireland no longer offers these lads the dream, let alone the opportunity, to succeed and flourish.

What I do know is that many of them will not come home. The reality is that mothers will lose their sons. Ireland will lose its future. And I still cannot answer the question of why we are doing this.

My heart already grieves for such loss.

With love and affection from your brother,

James

I wish I could talk to Eli about this, but he is indifferent, and even hostile, where James or the Irish are concerned.

I woke up to a winter sky, cloudless and stark blue. Eli was adding wood to the stove and the open door brought a gush of frigid air that made my nostrils hurt when I inhaled.

It was my home; we have three small children and we are on safe ground. Despite this, I felt unsettled since I had read the letter from James. I imagine the anguish these Irish mothers must feel as they send their sons to war. As we sat down for our morning coffee, I tried to share with him the sadness that such the European war was fostering in that country. Eli simply got up from the table and with cold eyes said, *I don't really care about what this so-called brother of yours thinks or the bloody mess they all have gotten themselves into over there, Margaret. They all deserve one another. Wilson better not tangle the rest of us into it is all I've got to say.*

And with that, he went into the barn, leaving me as wounded as the soldiers in the fields to come.

March

At Belle's apartment, the fiery political discussions around winning the vote have quieted. Most of our time is now spent on what we call the "the bread and butter issues" of turning our plan into a reality. Ideology has been replaced with practicalities.

We need to raise money for our barnstorming. The press, paper, printing and postage all come at a price. Travel is expensive—gasoline, hotels, meals. Publicity for the meetings is needed to gain popular support. Money is needed to move us forward. And though Belle and a few other advocates have been generous, it is not enough.

I am still not sure how it happened, but all at once I became the keeper of the purse. And we need to raise money. It is exhilarating and exhausting to be part of the central engine that is advancing our mission. And though I never thought there were enough hours in the day to get done all that I had to do, I find the time to commit to this.

May

It clearly gets my dander up the way the men treat me. Most of them act like I don't have a brain in my head. They either don't listen or talk over me—and not just me. It is true for most of my women friends, though it doesn't seem to irritate them as much as it does me.

I am really annoyed tonight, and my temper is flaring. It began last week, at the barn-raising at the Rushfords', where Eli and the men were complaining about the low prices they were getting for their milk. Seems like the owners at Queen City Dairy are negotiating with each of the individual farmers and agreeing on prices much lower than what is needed to run the farms.

As I was serving the pie, I asked why they all didn't pool their milk and sell directly to the businesses in Buffalo themselves. *Should be simple, just like we do when we go into East Aurora market on Wednesdays with our eggs.*

I told them I heard from one of the women in town that the farmers up near Syracuse had done this and it was working very well. She told me the dairy farmers there were getting much better prices by pulling together and forming a cooperative.

At first, no one paid any attention to what I said. So, I said it again.

Rushford just laughed and said to Eli: *Doesn't Margaret have enough to do with those children of yours to raise? Now she wants to run the farm, too? What will happen if she gets the vote as well?*

To Eli's credit, he said I had a good sense of the farm and he left all the bookkeeping to me as I was good with figures and "the like."

I wanted to put them all straight, that since I began keeping track of which chickens hatched what eggs and what cows gave which milk, we now know our best producers. That must be the "and the like" I am good at. Makes me so mad sometimes I see purple.

But I just went on cutting and serving the pies.

Then tonight, I couldn't believe my ears. Eli came home from a meeting at the church to tell me the men have decided to develop a cooperative: bringing all their milk together, so they can sell at a higher price. He was quite proud of the idea. He said the men were all energized about going right to the businesses and the shippers themselves to negotiate their prices.

Eli was strutting like a rooster. He had been selected to be one of the men to begin negotiations with the Buffalo businesses. He was all fired up about how they were going to break away from Queen City Dairy and act on their own behalf.

He acted as if it was all their idea. I wanted to shout at him that I was the one who suggested it to him and our neighbors over a week ago. But I held my tongue. I was just too tired to argue tonight. Better that I write my feelings in this journal and get on with life.

June

James continues to encourage my growing involvement in the suffragette movement. When I feel I have too much to do and not enough time to do it in, I reread his letters. His words, full of hope and commitment for an independent Ireland and for all men and women to have their own voice heard instills in me the greater sense of what needs to be done. They provide the fuel to keep me moving.

I am so thankful to have him in my life, even though he is many miles away.

July

Another debate at Belle's last night about whether this was the right time to pursue our cause. With our country on the brink of war—no matter what Wilson purports—some argued that we should put aside our suffrage movement until such troubles are over and the world at peace.

While James talks of the war and the travesties that fall on the streets of Ireland, I have never known its terrors. Both sides of the argument on whether we should postpone our efforts or go forth with our plan to capture the vote were equally compelling. I wasn't sure where I stood on the matter until Stella, who is a new friend of Belle's, raised her voice.

Stella has the bearing of the new woman who is touted in all the ladies' magazines. She is slender, athletic, and somewhat erotic, with cropped red-brownish hair that reminds me of the color of brewed tea. In her strong voice, clear and crisp, she brought us back to the issue at hand:

It is the militancy of men that has drenched this world with blood. And for such deeds of horror, these men have been lauded with monuments in our parks and with poems heralding them and their transgressions.

The militancy of women harms no human life except the lives of our sisters who want to fight the battle their own way. This is why we need to have our voices heard today. Not tomorrow. We are the flag bearers of sanity. We give birth to children. We will not hastily send them to their deaths on lands far from where they were born.

We must be given the right to vote. We must have our voices heard!

There was no comeback from anyone, but a nodding confirmation that what was just spoken was right. We settled back to finalize our action plan.

A small miracle has taken place at home. I think God has answered my prayer as to how I am to do all I need to. Sarah Rhoder, all of twelve years old, approached me after church on Sunday. She wants to learn to play the piano but was very clear she had no money to pay for the lessons. With her braids hanging down her back and eyes dark with determination far beyond her years, she said she was willing to barter her time as pay. She could come to the house after school to watch the children and on certain Saturdays. In return, she asked if I would teach her how to play.

Nothing would give me more pleasure, I responded. *And I will accept your offer, once I clear it with your mother.* As it turns out, her mother was surprised that Sarah had approached me, but with her a twinkle in her eyes, gave her approval with a nod and said, *Sarah is a bit like you, Margaret. All about books and business. Wouldn't be surprised if you turned her into a suffragette as well. Just don't have her go off marching down the streets of New York. Her father would have a heart attack!*

While I was a bit taken aback that I have been cast as a suffragette, I smiled to myself that I am getting such a reputation among my neighbors. We are doing important work. And with Sarah's help, my life will be just a bit easier.

August

What a day. Mary Macaulay and the suffragette entourage came to our church lawn fete this afternoon. We had handed out pamphlets and flyers announcing she was coming and most, men and women alike, could not curb their curiosity to see how one of "their own" had transformed into a national spokesperson for such a cause.

She handled the crowd beautifully. She talked with the women about their gardens and their children; she asked the men about their crops and the impact electricity has had on their farms. She told the children how she operates the press telegrapher for big city newspapers.

By the time she was ready to speak, all—from the youngest to the oldest, men and women alike—were ready to hear what she had to say.

Voting is more than a right we are asking for. It is our duty as Americans.

It is the duty of women to know that our water supplies, sanitary conditions, schools and hospitals are as they should be. The right to vote is a necessary tool to protect our families, our homes, and our children.

Giving women the ballot is not simply a matter of rights or even equality. Instead, it is a vital instrument of the work of women as mothers and caretakers of the farm and farm life.

The reaction of the women was immediate. They were all excitedly talking and laughing, creating a great buzz of female harmony.

The men seemed to catch the fever and many were soon waving pennants—that they had paid for—embellished with the words, "**Votes for Women**." It was exhilarating!

I looked for Eli in the crowd but couldn't find him.

As we were driving home that evening, I asked what he thought of Mary's speech. He told me he didn't have time to hear such prattle. There were issues with the cooperative and that was what was truly important. He and a group of other men had been meeting in the church basement during Mary's speech.

I will be glad when you get the vote so that all this foolishness will be over, was his only response.

Well, at least it sounds like we have his vote.

There is still so much to do. And it is harvest time!

November

My life would be easier if Eli looked to share in it. But he has routine, and it is his alone. As the light in the skies gets shorter, he leaves for the barn before dawn and the daylight is gone by the time he comes in for his supper. His mood is often as dark as the sky. I count the days until the sun wakes us up and remains in the heaven longer than the stars. But that is months away and there is much to be done in getting ready for the winter.

Sarah has been a wonderful help and the children look forward to her coming. I believe they think she is their big sister. She is gifted at the piano and I take as much pleasure in showing her how to make music as she does in learning how to make the ivories respond to her touch.

The legacy of Mrs. Brown continues now in my parlor.

April

As of the 6th of this month, we are at war.

How I tremble at the thought of our young men crossing the sea and fighting the likes of which they have never seen.

Belle speaks of life in Buffalo, where the opinions and rhetoric being touted make the blood boil and spirits rise. Young men are inspired, signing up to take part in this "Great War." Sheldon is a village that is generally well-informed, but never completely up-to-date. Here, our passions are more a slow simmer. Yet as any good cook knows, a slow simmer can generate just as much heat underneath a pot of stew as a burning flame.

May

I cannot sleep. Images of this afternoon keep flooding my

mind. I heard Louise scream, and every mother knows the sound of their child in danger rather than at play.

I was at the kitchen table, engrossed in finalizing the numbers from the upcoming *Get Out the Vote* campaign, when I heard terrible shrieking coming from the chicken coop. Skirts flying, I found my way into the yard to see Louise being attacked by one of the roosters. He was crowing as he picked at her head, jabbing her with his claws, beating her with his wings. Louise was trying to pull away, but her flailing arms seemed to agitate him more.

I yelled for Eli as I scooped Louise up in my arms, my heart beating so fast I could hear it. I kicked the rooster with all my might just as Eli came running from the barn. He picked the rooster up, and in one quick motion flung it across the yard, breaking its neck.

Louise stopped crying, looking at her father, her protector, and reached out her arms saying: *Daddy, you saved me.* Eli engulfed her, his hands stroking the hair that only minutes ago had been the rooster's mark. *Always, my little love,* he cooed. *I will never let anyone or anything harm my little girl.*

My heart filled with the picture of the two of them in that moment. Rarely emotional and seldom comforting, here Eli was both.

As he handed her back to me to take her inside, he muttered, *you should have been out here with her, Margaret. That is your role, not bent over some book of numbers for women and a cause I don't care a lick about.*

And with that, he stomped into barn without so much as a look backward.

Feelings of guilt, anger, and disbelief flooded me. The loving picture I had just witnessed had been erased.

Louise is fine. I am not.

June

James writes that the American Navy arrived in full force in Queenstown in May. Upon their arrival in Cork, it appears that only the ladies of the town welcomed these sailors with open arms. The local gents would have none of the women beguiled by the likes of such Yanks. They attacked the sailors, and more than one of the shore party was sent back to their ship with heads bashed and limbs broken.

Eventually, the US sailors were made to stay on their ships as the newspapers heralded them to be, "overpaid, oversexed, and over there." Even in times such as these, there are headlines that make me chuckle.

My guess is that fighting is in the Irish blood whether it is for their lands or their lassies.

September

Men do, however, seem to fight over the silliest things. Whether the Georges are German or French seems to be an issue at most family gatherings. From what I have been able to gather, the German branch looks to Charlemagne as their forbearer, while the French branch raises the flag of Louis XIV.

Eli and my father could get all worked up when the talk came to the Franco-Prussian War when the Germans gained control of their language, their politics, and their culture. They recalled the fighting the battles won or lost so long ago as if it were yesterday.

I believe the fighting on the fields of Europe is a continuation of nursing these same old wounds and revenging slights from the past. The monarchs who dictate that young boys must take up arms for some notion of fighting for a greater cause are no better suited than our neighboring farmers in finding peaceful solutions to the troubles that now face us all.

I pray that Stella is right: once women have the vote, there will be more talk of peace than of war.

The hours and work I am putting into the movement astound even me. Yet I feel more energized and engaged than ever before. Fighting for what is right seems to add hours on the day, although the time between when I crawl under the sheets and the dawn is shorter and shorter.

My involvement seems to go unnoticed at home, now that Eli and our neighboring farmers are starting their own cooperative to compete with the Buffalo dairy distributors. As a result, he is often away, and the timing couldn't be better for me as he is distracted and unconcerned about what time I arrive at our marital bed.

November 6th

An historic day I will never forget. Women in New York can vote!

I am so excited I can barely write the news. The statewide

referendum passed, and New York is the first East Coast state to allow women to have their voices heard at the ballot box.

I am over the moon.

Our petition served as the catalyst for the vote. In the end, we had over a million signatures. Belle is having a big party to celebrate.

Days later...

The past two days are like a mosaic in the making: different pieces, colorful and shiny, but whose finished outcome I cannot foresee.

I am confused. No, perhaps "bewildered" is the better way to describe it. It is good that I have this journal to capture my thoughts or else I might go quite mad.

The celebration at Belle's was going to be fun. Simply fun. We all knew each other so well that there was comfort in being able to be ourselves, with no roles to play: wife, mother, or church-goer. We had worked hard together, not always easily, but the evening was about celebrating, and we were all in unison on that front.

The day dawned well, the kind of late autumn day that I love. The sun was trying gallantly to warm the land as the distant graying clouds foretold of winter's looming arrival.

Sarah and her mother were staying at the house, so I had no worries that the children would be well taken care of. As I made my way to Belle's, I watched geese in perfect formation make their way to warmer skies and wondered what it would be like to be that free.

Belle's buffet dinner was sumptuous and the cider so fresh you could taste the crisp, ripe apples from which it sprang. After the food was served, Belle put on the gramophone, and we all started practicing dances that sounded more like barnyard than ballroom: the Foxtrot, the Bunny Hop, the Turkey Trot. We flapped our arms, shook our shoulders, stomped our feet, wiggled our backsides.

I paused to catch my breath, exhausted and exhilarated. At the evening's end, hair uncoiled and dresses stained with perspiration, we embraced and hugged each other, agreeing that we would meet next at the ballot box.

In the guest room, I woke in the middle of the night, and got up to get a glass of water. As I turned to go back, I saw Stella leaving Belle's bedroom. She was naked, her crumpled clothes nestled in her bare arms. She didn't see me, and I scurried back to the safety of my sanctuary.

As I fell back to sleep, I wasn't sure I had actually seen Stella leaving Belle's room or had merely dreamt it. Given the amount of cider I'd consumed, I was sure it could be the after-effect of too many glasses raised in celebration.

In the morning, I crept out from under the covers, shook off the feelings of doubt from the night before, and left the room.

Shortly thereafter, any question about what had happened that night was answered. As I made my way to the staircase, Belle's door was ajar. Stella and Belle were standing there, locked in an embrace, kissing each other. And, not as sisters. Stella was running her hands from Belle's back to her neck.

Stone-like, I stood mesmerized and in shock. Belle moaned and swayed into Stella's taut frame as she began to kiss the spot below Belle's upturned chin. Backing away, I stumbled to my room, not knowing whether the heat on my face was from shame, embarrassment, or arousal.

I stared out the window until I heard them say their goodbyes and the front door close. Only then did I feel I could safely leave.

Belle was sitting at the kitchen table, still in her dressing gown, when I entered the room. She quickly began to chatter about what a great party it had been. I could find no words to respond. Then Belle stopped talking and looked at me. *What's wrong, Margaret? You haven't said a word to me, and your tea cup has grown cold in your hand.*

This was Belle, whom I loved as dearly as I loved anyone in my life. I had to tell her what I saw. Faltering and unable to look at that face I knew so well, I told her I had seen her with Stella, and that I had seen Stella leave her room last night.

Belle sighed as she took my hand. *So, that's all.*

That's all? Belle, what you are doing is a sin! You will go to hell.

She held my hand tighter as she looked into my eyes: *Margaret, do you believe God is a loving God?*

I nodded.

So do I. And he gives us people in our life that we are to love. For me, I am in love with a man who died too early and with a woman who is very much alive. I believe God wants us to love whomever we want, however we want. Don't you agree?

Again, only a nod.

It is about love, Margaret. Stella makes me happy, content. She is the first person I want to see in the morning and the last person I want to see at night. It is in her arms I find comfort. It is in her eyes I see the beauty of who I am. It is the same love that you must feel for Eli.

I could not respond.

I am not sure I understand the love that Belle describes, though I don't doubt for a minute it is what she feels for Stella. The love she and John shared was so powerful you felt their bond when you were in their presence. She could not settle for less, even now.

I love Eli, I clearly do. But it is not the kind of love Belle describes. Our life is a tapestry where nothing changes but the seasons. Our love is woven together by threads of family, church, farm, and friends. Belle's life is more like the watercolors painted by those Impressionist painters she adores —full of color, bold strokes, and imaginary places. I am comfortable being with Eli; I know what to expect and when to expect it. I don't have the love that Belle describes, and there is an emptiness in the realization that something is missing.

I looked at Belle, who had been so many things to me for all the years: defender, promoter, and mentor. So much of what is good in my life, I owe to her. I replied: *You are my sister. Whomever you love and however you love...well, it is nobody's business but your own.*

Belle threw back her head and laughed her own special laugh. *Good, now that we have settled that, it's time to get you a proper cup of tea.*

And she did.

I have no intention of telling Eli about Belle and Stella. I think this is the first secret I have knowingly kept from him.

I wonder if it will be my last.

December

Choir practice last night brought a sense of peace to my troubled mind. Funny, how a bit of singing brings each of us together as one. There we were in our own worlds, with our own problems, and then suddenly they seemed to dissolve. Our voice blending, each of us doing our part—supporting each other, not only in song, but in our daily lives.

Sarah accompanied the choir for one of the hymns. I could not tell who was prouder of her at that moment: me or her mother. She has a natural talent and maturity beyond her years, and it is lovely to be a part of it all.

Women create a bond with each other that may get stretched and sometimes grows threadbare, but it's always there.

That is what counts.

January

The distrust of those of us with German-sounding names and backgrounds has taken a turn the likes we have never seen before.

Belle had told us stories of volunteer watchdog groups that were reporting on the activities of German-Americans throughout Buffalo. Initially, we laughed when she told us sauerkraut was now being called "liberty cabbage." Now, it has lost any semblance of humor as we learned that Schmidt's Gardens, one of Eli's favorite taverns, is being boycotted with threatening slurs painted on its doors.

Our own peace-loving President is fueling this fire of prejudice. The papers reported on his recent speech: *The military masters of Germany . . . have filled our unsuspecting communities with vicious spies and conspirators.*

Our friends and family are being treated as enemies, yet most were born here. I am happy that Father is not alive to witness this. How proud he was to be an American! But with his accent and foreign ways, who knows how he would be treated today.

Loyalty is now being judged by the purchase of war bonds, singing nationalistic songs, and declarations of allegiance to the American flag. Any civilized discussion on whether or not we should have entered into this war is seen as being unpatriotic or worse.

Even more concerning, it is assumed that because you have German forefathers, you must be cheering for the Kaiser to be victorious. Such foolishness—as if anyone could support that little man in his soldier's uniform adorned with unearned medals.

Leon doesn't understand what is happening for he is only a child. I understand only too well.

Eli came in last night while Leon was playing soldier with a found tree limb for his rifle. While he was singing that silly song, *You're in the army now, you're not behind the plow. You'll never get rich by digging a ditch . . .* " Eli walked into the room, poured a cup of coffee and stared at his young son as he took his first sip. After taking another swallow of the steaming brew, he slammed the cup on the table and grabbed Leon by the shoulder. Something in his burning eyes frightened me.

I never want to hear that song in this house, young man, Eli shouted as Leon began to sob. I pulled Leon to me, *He's only a child,* I cried, *it's only a silly song. He doesn't know what it means.*

Well, he'd better learn that being behind the plow is his destiny. Stop coddling him, Margaret. He is growing into a Mama's boy. And with that he, stormed out of the kitchen.

I wiped away Leon's tears and held him. I wish there was a way I could get Eli to show Leon the same type of love and affection he showers on Louise, and only Louise.

February

Both in Europe and at home, we have become victims of brutality.

Belle and Stella were visiting this afternoon when they told me the most horrific news. Alice Paul and the other Suffragettes, while demonstrating for the universal right for women to vote in every state, were arrested and taken to a prison in Virginia where they were violently beaten. While neither Belle nor I approved of their tactics—calling the President "Kaiser Wilson"—they certainly shouldn't have been victimized.

The papers described the women being thrown into cold, unsanitary, and rat-infested cells. Led by Alice Paul, they staged a hunger strike and were then forcibly fed in a tortuous method. And the headlines shout that these women are the ones insane!

This is all too crazy. Are not the fields of Europe stained with the blood of boys fighting for freedom? And shouldn't women be free as well? It sometimes seems too much. I am not sure where the world is going.

To add to my despair, James writes of a brutality in Ireland that I cannot even imagine.

My Dear Sister,

While the fields of Europe remain covered with the blood and bodies of young men from everywhere, our own Ireland has a police force so cruel that its name defines murder, brutality and massacre. They are the Black and Tans—men who kill and destroy on a large scale without regard for the sanctity of life or the code of justice. Their odd name comes about by the look of their uniforms—a motley mixture of army khaki and black police tunics, all hastily put together by the Crown. They have been given the mandate to quell our fight to govern this land, a land that is rightfully ours.

The Tans appear to have neither religion nor a moral compass. In the foulest language, they refer to us as 'natives' as they steal from us whenever and however they choose. Our clergy and many of their own generals denounce them as savages, yet they have abandoned all civility when dealing with our people, terrorizing women and children for no reason.

One of their commanders was reported in the papers to

give the following order: "The more you shoot, the better I will like you, and I assure you no policeman will get into trouble for shooting any man. Innocent persons may be shot, but that cannot be helped, and you are bound to get the right parties some time." What words are those from a man who calls himself a Christian?

What the British have never understood is that the more reprisals there are against Irish civilians, the more our revolutionaries will increase their call to arms.

Violence will foster more violence and our children may never know peace. I predict the reputation of the Black and Tans will serve forever as the hallmark of British violence and Irish victimhood for years to come, not only on this Island but across the sea in America.

Given my position at the bank and the neighborhood in which we live, I do not fear for my life or for my family. I do, however, weep for this land that I love. The blood of too many is being spilt by the brutality of this group of thugs.

With a sad heart, but one filled with love and affection for you,

Your brother,

James

March

As the War takes our children from our farms, we are now destroying our heritage. Along with our neighbors, we burned all our books written in German.

Father brought many of them with him when he came over to this country, and Eli had Bibles that have been in his family for generations. But to keep such items in our homes is seen as unpatriotic, as if that was the test of loyalty of our love for this country.

The night was cold and windless when we set the bonfire. Other neighbors came with their sacrifices to the flame. This was not a celebration, but, like Joan of Arc, a death by fire.

It was an odd gathering. A shroud of despair covered the group and few words were spoken. The pages ignited quickly as if they, too, wanted to escape all that what was happening.

I watched as people moved farther away from the heat of the flames, trying to find a spot where they were comfortable. But even while our faces burned hot, our backs were cold as the late winter winds swirled around us.

Eventually, Eli took the children home, but I could not leave. I stepped closer and closer until I could no longer tolerate the heat. When I looked around, the ring of people was far behind me. I was alone at the edge of the fire watching the books go up in smoke.

I felt the world as we know it was being consumed by these same leaping flames. I am unsure as to what phoenix will arise from these ashes. All I could see was the gateway to hell.

That night in the comfort of our bed, I turned to Eli, feeling his confusion and despair. *I don't know what this world is coming to, Margaret,* he choked out. *We burned the word of God tonight because they were written in a different language. No one would have ever doubted the loyalty of my father to this country, his church or his family. Why is this happening to me?*

To us? Where is the humanity? I held him tight as I whispered, *I don't know.*

August

The early summer mornings are my own time. I walk into the garden and watch the dew slowly disappear on the colorful petals of the flowers. As I gently pull the weeds away, I smell the ripening vegetables and feel a contentment that will soon be edged away by the demands of the day. But for these few precious moments, the land is mine and I have my feet firmly planted on it. Before the heat of the day takes away my breath, the breeze is gentle and fresh and mine alone.

September

I cannot remember Ireland, but James describes a land so beautiful that I can see it clearly when I close my eyes.

My Dear Maggie,

We have just returned from a weekend in the southwest of Ireland, a much-needed respite from the talk and tribulations of war.

Whilst Dublin has a beauty and charm of its own, you must venture outside the City and environs to understand why it is a land that so many have fought over for so many centuries. It was a special holiday, celebrating the end of term for Jimmy who has succeeded beyond our expectations in his studies.

Our destination was a small cottage in the Dingle

Peninsula, where we could explore, relax and enjoy each other's company. The weather was fine, a gift that is rare as the days grow shorter.

Each day began with Jimmy and me climbing down the dunes and seeing our footprints leave their marks in the pristine sand. The coastline was rugged and deserted. We were the Vikings of old, arriving on unexplored shores in search of adventure and tales to tell.

There was nothing but sky melting into the brine. Blue upon blue. The color only broken by the passing clouds and waves rising to greet each other. And yet with the pounding of the sea and the surf, the air around us was quite still. It was as if you were standing in awe in one of the great cathedrals. You speak in a whisper, finding a sense of peace in the majesty that surrounds you.

These are the parts of Ireland that are so remote and so mystifying, so wind-slammed and sea-tossed, so hilly and so green that they fill your senses. Nature composes its own symphony: a composition for the pounding sea accompanied by the birds crying and the whipping winds blowing the surf to shore. And we are its only audience.

Jimmy and I could only stand and embrace the love of this land that we call home.

This all makes me aware of how small a part my life plays in this grand universe. It brings my spirit to rest in a way nothing else can. I can scream as loud as I want and yet no sound can compete with the unbroken thrashing of the sea on the sand. I raise my face to the sun and say a prayer of thanksgiving more fervent than any I have said whilst on my knees.

We are an Island—untamed and untamable.

This is Ireland. We are Irish. And it is grand.

With love and affection,

Your brother

James

October

Well, the Schmidts are now on par with the King and Queen of England in denouncing their German heritage. George V, by his own decree, changed his family's Germanic surname of "Saxe-Coburg-Gotha" to "Windsor."

James writes that the Crown has very little loyalty to their family. And such a clan it is: married to his German cousin, King George is at war with the Kaiser and Czar Nicholas of Russia, all his first cousins. Family picnics must be a real treat with this group.

The Schmidts, fearing retribution from the anti-German sentiment swirling around the countryside, are now to be called "Smith." Their young son christened "Manfred" is now "Maynard."

Mr. "Smith" made the announcement of the family name change after church on Sunday. There was a bit of muttering from some of the men, but I am more sympathetic. I, too, have had to give up my name and my heritage in order to be accepted.

Eli failed to make the connection. When I pressed the point, he shrugged and said my circumstances were different: I was a woman and Irish. Very different than being German and a man.

Sometimes he makes my blood boil, but I stay calm.

November 5th—an historic day

As I got dressed to cast my ballot, I could barely speak for the excitement of it all.

Sarah came over to stay with the children as Eli and I prepared to go to vote. She seemed excited to be part of the experience and we chatted as we fed the children their breakfast.

You will not have to fight for this privilege. Our daughters and their daughters will take voting for whom and what they please to be as natural as the morning frost on the fields, telling us that winter is on its way. But you must tell them that it was a battle worth the fight and a right that they must never take for granted. I turned to Louise and Florence, though too young to understand what I was saying, and added: *It will be up to you to remember that your Aunt Belle and I took up the banner to make this happen for you.*

Sarah said she was looking forward to the day that she could cast her first ballot. With solemn eyes, she added, *I will vote in every election as long as I am able. And for whom and what I think is right.*

I smiled back, *Exactly, Sarah. That is why we worked and why so many risked so much for this privilege.*

Eli just listened during this conversation making no comment on what we're saying. I am not sure those who have always been able to vote would ever understand how empowering it is to know that you finally have a say in how things are run. I uttered a silent prayer that the next generations of women never fall into that same nonchalance. May they all be like Sarah.

Belle and Stella were in front of the village hall handing out fliers of *What Every Woman Needs to Know About Voting*. Bella approached each woman with the challenge: *Now that we got the vote, we must learn to use it.*

She laughed as she approached Eli. *Would you like a copy, brother of mine?* His initial look of puzzlement turned to annoyance, and he cuffed her hand to move the paper away. *We're just here to vote, Belle. Margaret has more to do with her days than idly hand out sheets of paper to folks who should already know what to do with their vote. Wasn't that what all the hullaballoo was about in the first place?*

Stella spoke up, the first time I had ever heard her respond to him directly. *Oh, and the hullabaloo isn't over yet, Eli. Just last week, women were clubbed, beaten and tortured after they were arrested for practicing what should be their First Amendment right of free speech, expressing their desire to be have their voices heard. What you call a hullabaloo, we are calling the Night of Terror. All women want is to vote, the same as you.*

And with that, she turned away to the next gathering of women coming to exercise this newly found freedom to be heard.

Eli guffawed. *Well such shenanigans didn't happen here in*

Sheldon. No one got arrested when you were asking for the vote. You got what you wanted and should be happy that the men in this State agreed. He then took my hand and led me to the table to cast my ballot.

I voted for Al Smith for Governor. To think he is Irish-Catholic makes this day even more momentous. I am proud to be Irish, even if I have to keep it to myself. As I voted, I said a prayer for all those women who were being punished so cruelly for wanting the right to vote. Like the choir, our voices come in unison, for we are one together.

November 11: Armistice Day

The war is over.

Our prayers are answered.

May this truly be the war to end all wars.

January

The Dentons have lost their only son, Otto, to the war effort. I remember how proud he was to join up, showing his family's patriotism in the midst of all the animosity in the air. He was but 17 years old.

This past week, I saw Mr. Denton at the market and commented I had not seen him or his family in church. He looked at me and spat:

We should pray to God? For what? Our boy was taken from us and not on the battlefield. He survived the machine-gun fire and the barbed wire, but died from the flu. The flu! There were no doctors to administer to my boy and his comrades as they lay dying. Hundreds of them. They should have been on their way home. The Armistice had been signed.

The arrogance, stupidity and pigheadedness of politicians and generals killed my boy. They should be tried as murderers, for they caused his death as surely as the epidemic that spread throughout his camp.

I cannot forgive them. I have nothing left to pray for.

And with that, he stormed away.

Such sadness. War takes so much from us, our children, our sense of security, our hope for the future. I don't know if I could manage without my faith. If I turned away from God, I am not sure what direction I would be heading.

February

Winter feels endless this year. Gusts rattle the windows, and frost has found its way inside their panes. We are isolated in this land of white and ice. The earth is frozen solid and the clouds so gray they make you shiver at their sight. I am not sure I will ever feel the warmth of the sun on my back again. I ache to be in my garden.

March

I am pregnant again and feeling quite despondent that this is my only role in life, to have children. Then I hear from James and my world gets brighter. He rekindles in me the spark of being my own woman, with my own ideas and thoughts.

Why I would never want to be this Countess, it is heartening to know that someone, somewhere is proud of me. And perhaps I have a bit of spunk in me as well, though there is not much left of me at the end of day to find it.

My Dear Sister,

You fought hard to gain women the right the vote to vote in New York and I thought I would introduce you to an Irish woman that shares your spunk and determination here in Ireland, though her background has more than a few rough patches.

Countess Constance Georgine Markievicz is revolutionary, a nationalist and a suffragette. She is also a gaolbird who is the first women named to the government's cabinet as the Minister of Labour. No small feat and I am quite proud that our government is the first to place a woman in such a key role, particularly a woman that has such a firebrand reputation.

Countess Constance is the daughter of an English-Irish lord Sir Henry Gore-Booth and has made quite a name for herself in this land and with the Crown. While you may not share her passion for guns and mortar, you are kindred spirits in standing up for what you believe to be right.

Though there is some question as to whether or not her husband had a true noble claim, the Countess donned the title as soon as their marriage was recognized. It was then that the two of them began making inroads with those Dubliners who shared their artistic and literary bent. The concern and preservation of the Irish language and culture brought both sides of the nationalist divide to their gatherings and it was here that the Countless became actively involved in Irish politics. She subsequently joined up with the likes of the actress Maud Gonne in the revolutionary women's movement and the two were quite the sensation on and off the stage. The Count left for his homeland and has not been heard from since.

Our Uncle, who met the Countess early on, told the story of her spoiling a political rally of an English aristocrat by the name of Winston Churchill who was ardently opposed to the women's suffragette movement. She was driving an old-fashioned carriage drawn by four white horses to advertise the cause for women's right to vote. In the crowd was a male heckler who shouted out if she could cook a dinner, to which she responded, "Yes. Can you drive a coach and four?" The laughter overtook any of the political musings Mr. Churchill was hoping to deliver. Uncle Andrew would chuckle as he told the story, adding that he loved the spunk of Irish women, no matter what church they bowed their head in. In due time, the Countess left the Church of Ireland and converted to Catholicism. It would have made our Uncle love her even more.

The Countess's political reputation was forged during the Easter Rising in 1916. Captured by the Crown for the alleged killing of an English policeman, she escaped the death penalty of fellow patriots by the sheer fact that she was a woman. According to the newspapers, when she learned her fate, she turned to her captors and said: "I do wish your lot had the decency to shoot me." Her sex may have saved her life but she never lets her gender interfere in doing what she believes to be the right thing to do.

Even while imprisoned, her political ties and aspirations were not quelled. This year, she was the first women elected to the House of Commons in London, though there is some question as to whether she will take her seat.

If the headlines are correct, the women in your country will soon gain the right to vote no matter what state they live. The restriction in Ireland (and throughout all of Great Britain) grants only a sliver of our female population the right to cast a ballot. My own Annie, one of the smartest and best-formed people I know, cannot cast the ballot because she is not a property owner nor possesses a university education. Perhaps when Ireland is a free nation, we will right this wrong. Until then, may the States lead the way and give every man and woman the right to make their voice heard at the ballot box.

Keep up the fight, my dear sister. Not with guns and bullets but with your convictions and energy to make a difference in this world for our children. I am very proud of you.

With love and affection.

Your brother,

James

April

It is the most extraordinary thing. We have a new priest in the parish, and he is from Ireland!

Father Joseph, who has been here seemingly forever, is leaving, and Father Michael has come to take his place.

The lilt I had worked so hard to lose flows easily from his lips, and the parish seems enthralled when he speaks. Even Belle had to laugh when she came to visit and heard his first sermon.

Well Margaret, looks like I won't need to put up fists to save his honor. The ladies seem quite charmed by his brogue, though I understand the good priest studied in London prior to returning home to take his vows, so his voice is a bit gentler on our ears.

I reminded her that was years ago, and the World War seemed to make people more tolerant of those who look or sound different.

But not too different, she chortled, as she made her way over to Stella's side.

Father Michael has the dark Irish looks I so link to my image of James: coal-black hair with eyes the color of Dresden blue. When we were first introduced, those eyes actually twinkled as he looked down at me: *I hear we have a homeland in common, Mrs. George. From what your good priest has told me, you arrived in this parish from Ireland not so many years ago yourself.*

It had been so long since I thought about anyone calling me Irish I was at a loss for words. The sound of his voice stirred ghosts from my past.

And where was your land?

I found my senses by then and replied, *Cork, though so long ago I have nothing but shadow memories. I do have a brother who lives in Dublin, though I have not seen him since we left. He writes to tell me of the struggles past and present that the country still faces.*

He smiled: *I am a Belfast man, myself. Sadly, we Catholics remain hostages, being denied our basic rights that you in this country enjoy—even the women. Now what would be your views on how the Irish are looked upon here in Sheldon and beyond? We should be finding time in the next days to have a proper chat over a cup of tea.*

I nodded somewhat foolishly. That a man would seek my opinion about anything was astonishing. And that he was a priest, almost unheard of. But I do feel a bit full of myself that I was singled out by this newcomer to our small town.

I told him he should call me "Margaret," as it was the custom in our parish. Father Michael smiled and said that he would like to participate in our choir practice, if it was alright with me. I told him he would be welcomed.

He gave me a sidelong glance and asked: *Do any call you 'Maggie?' I know of few Irish colleens who call themselves 'Margaret;' most go by 'Maggie,' including my wee favorite cousin.*

I replied*: Only my brother.*

So, it is, he replied. *If it sits well with you, in public I shall call you 'Margaret' but in our own conversations, it shall be 'Maggie.' It will make me slightly less wistful for the hills and lakes of my beloved home.*

I mumbled something incoherently, called for the children, and found my way to the car, feeling somehow like a schoolgirl, all tongue-tied and confused. And as I replied, I believe there was a slight lilt in my voice as well.

May

Florence is over three and is my delight. I smile when I am in her presence. Her hair is like Nell's, soft auburn curls, and even at this young age, she has a mind of her own. She has my eyes, my link to Ma and to Nell. I would deny loving any of my children more than the others, but perhaps I treasure her a bit more than the other two.

Louise, on the other hand, defies me at every turn. She is just turning five. When I try to discipline her, she runs sobbing to Eli, who always seems to take her side. They are thick as thieves.

It is Leon, now just 7, who is left out. A loner, he seeks no hand to hold or lap to sit in. I don't know if it is his natural temperament, or that Eli and I have made our choices and no one selected him.

August

There is a pattern to life on the farm that provides a sense of security in its rhythms. Harvesting brings neighbors across the fields to help each other. Each of us has our role: our husbands, our children, our horses. Each of us is doing what we must do make the harvest successful. Our lives clearly depend upon it.

I see how the cycle has moved by looking at my children. It

feels like only yesterday Leon was walking beside me, his legs sturdy but unsteady as I served the men and the hired help their lunches. Then, as if overnight, he was taking water and lemonade to them in the field, without a look back at me. Albeit reluctantly, now he is leading the horses, helping to bring in the grain—more man than boy. The task of water boy is delegated to his younger cousin. Meanwhile, in the house, Louise is covered from head-to-toe with flour as she demands to learn how to make the pies for *Papa*. She is most content when she is in the kitchen playing *Mama*. I am not sure I am the best model for the role, but I will have to suffice.

And in the midst of all of that is known and expected, I seem to be growing more and more unsettled with the limits of what I can and cannot do, simply because I am a woman. Working to get women the vote seems so long ago. But it was then that I felt the most alive, that the world was an exciting place to be a part of.

September

Father Michael has begun coming to choir practice. He has a strong tenor voice that blends well with the others, and I find myself looking forward to seeing him as much as I do hearing our voices united in song.

Even in the most trying times, the choir brings me a sense of peace. It is funny how a bit of singing binds us together. We arrive focusing on our own sets of problems, and then suddenly everything seems to dissolve. As the first notes are sung, we realize we are here now, living through whatever joy or sorrow has come our way, blending our voices as we lift this one song to God.

The war has been over these many months, but the scars are still so visible. Elsie, an early schoolmate of mine, saw her three boys sign up to join the war as soon as they were able. Only two made it home: one has lost his leg; the other is unable to face living. She says their nights are full of terrors, their dreams haunted by dead friends. They are overwhelmed by guilt that they were allowed to live while so many died for no reason.

Awful as it sounds, I think it is easier to comfort those mothers whose sons never left the fields of Flanders. I cannot find the words to bring relief to Elsie and her boys. Some scars of the battlefront cannot be seen and cannot be healed. Her boys are simply wasting away with the memories of the horrors they have seen.

This must be the War that ends war. If not, all we have lost is in vain.

November

Leon seems to be all arms and legs that sprout without any regard for where they will end. While Eli is sturdy and stocky, like the maple tree in the backyard, Leon is the willow. Even now, he bends with the wind while never having the roots needed to secure him firmly to the earth. The land does not hold him as it does his father.

Yesterday, Leon spent the afternoon playing soldier rather than doing his chores. Eli was furious and sent him to bed without supper.

This morning as he was leaving for school, Leon expressed no remorse for his behavior. He told me he wished the war was still going on, so he could grow up to be a soldier and move to France. I told him he is too young to be talking such foolishness.

December

We have a new baby, another boy to be baptized Walter, who came much sooner than expected. He let out such a cry when he took his first breath that I knew all was well. Eli is pleased, another son. I smiled when he bent over him for the first time, checking out the ten fingers and ten toes.

They are all there, I chuckled. *He is fine and strong, just a bit small for coming this early.* Eli smiled, *Well done, my dear. It shall be a Merry Christmas indeed.*

I fell back to sleep with the silent prayer that I hoped he was right. May Walter be the son that makes Eli happy and brings peace to the house.

February

I wish I could write in this journal more often. It helps me keep my life orderly, gives me the release I need. There are just not enough hours in the day. With the washing and cooking for the older children, the hired men, and keeping the baby nursed and bathed, the day is done before I even know it has begun. There are days I simply don't know if I can carry on one more moment.

I remember when Lillian Martin ran off with that traveling salesman a couple of years ago and left her husband and three kids all alone. All of Sheldon was shocked that a wife and mother could do such a thing.

I can understand why she would run away. But there is no leaving my children.

I tried to talk to Eli about how I was feeling. As I started the conversation, he said, *Not now, Margaret. I have work to do.* And he left for the barn. That night when he started to reach for me in our bed, I said, *Not tonight, Eli.* He pulled away, saying, *Oh, that time of the month, heh?* He rolled over on his side and immediately went to sleep.

I curled up, hugging my knees into my chest. I lay there, eyes open, wanting to be held, to feel I was not alone. Exhaustion soon took over and I fell into a restless slumber.

March

James lives in a world where man's inhumanity to man is ever-present. Yet he seems able to feel a compassion for others that warms my heart.

Eli, however, deals in absolutes. His world is black and white, right and wrong, good and bad. In this way, he is assured of his world and his place in it. Some men, however, are not as fortunate as they ride the trains in search of work and a hot meal.

More than once, a man has approached the house hat-in-hand. Often, I am the only one at home with the children. I offer a meal for a task to be completed, usually a chore Leon is refusing to perform. I know men, even those down on their luck, have their pride. Never once have I feared for my safety or for that of the children.

The first time it happened, Eli was less than pleased, particularly when he found out the man had left with two loaves of my freshly baked bread and a jar of strawberry jam.

No preaching to me, I retorted. *It is just a meal and we won't go hungry by our sharing it with others.*

Then he started on how they were nothing but beggars.

And what of Jesus? I asked.

He looked at me as if I were losing my mind. *What are you talking about, Margaret? What has Jesus got to do with these hobos?*

Did He not wander? I asked. *Did not his disciples have to fetch the bread and fishes he multiplied to feed the crowds?*

At this, he shook his head, and told me I could do whatever I wanted, but to mind the children. As if they are not my first priority.

I am not sure how many I have fed since the first one. Most days, I keep a pot of soup on the stove, so I have something easily on hand if I need to give a meal.

Last week, I noticed there was a cat drawn in charcoal on the fence. I had not seen it before, and it was clearly not something the children or their friends were likely to have done. I mentioned it to Father Michael at choir practice, and he smiled, the smile that sends shivers up my spine.

The hobos have a culture all their own, he told me. *In this country, some believe the word is a contraction of 'homeward bound' dating back to your Civil War when the soldiers worked their way home after the surrender.*

Over time, these hobos created a language of signs and symbols just like our early Christians. Their drawings are found in inconspicuous places but serve to communicate messages to their fellow drifters who would come later. A cat such as this means a kindhearted woman lives here. So, now the whole world knows what we know—Margaret George has a kind and loving heart.

I smiled and thanked him for both the bit of knowledge and the compliment. I know I have a heart—it feels like it is about to burst when I am with him.

June

My days are full, but not complete.

The tasks never-ending: scrubbing floors, washing linens, making meals. Daily duties interrupted only by the mundane chores of nose-wiping, clothes-mending and bread-kneading. I feel as if my head is both huge and empty, like a large balloon ready to burst. I want to pound the walls and scream.

I escape to the barn and do just that. No one sees or hears me. The birds in the rafters flap their wings in dismay and take flight with no looking down. No one seems to care. Particularly Eli.

November

Father Michael clearly has a way with the children. I have never seen so many of them participate in the Christmas Pageant before. He came to all three of the children's practices and was both funny and encouraging to even the most struggling youngster—and that would be Leon. He told them:

It is your heart more than your voice that makes the music. Jesus needs to hear your song, and when He does, He smiles. You see, He knows that you are singing just for Him. So let it rip, fellas. Don't hold back, the Lord is waiting.

From that moment on, the boys were energetic and cooperative, two things I had not witnessed before Father Michael's arrival. At the end of the last practice, he gave each child a piece of candy to thank them for all their hard work. They were over the moon.

Later, he walked me and the children to our car and with a wink and a whisper said: *Maggie, Joey Victor is a fine young lad, but he wouldn't be able to carry a tune if you put it in a bucket. Come Monday, I will announce our narrator for the Pageant.*

I nodded and laughed, but his nearness made me blush. I hurried the children into their seats, but I could not calm down the feeling of his being so close to me. It was the smell of him that would not leave me. It reminded of me of how the trees smell after a rain storm, clean and strong.

I am not sure these thoughts are sinful, but I won't be sharing them with anyone. Not even Belle.

And then I hear from James the most horrific news. With the war over, I thought that the world would embrace peace. Clearly, I was wrong.

My Dear Sister,

If I have the calendar right, you should be preparing for your Thanksgiving Day celebration. I am not sure that this letter will reach you before then. I am sad to write we have little to give thanks for in Dublin these days.

I doubt that American papers are reporting it, but this past Sunday, 21 November, will be known in the old language as 'Dominic an Foal,' a Bloody Sunday.

All told, 32 dead—from British soldiers to civilians.

The sadness started with a plan by Michael Collins, one of our rebel leaders against the Crown, to assassinate British agents around this City. There is still confusion and disagreement about what transpired, but from what I have been able to glean, of the fourteen agents killed all but one were either British spies or informers. Like scared rabbits, the Crown's lackeys fled to Dublin Castle to find safety in their special hole.

Later that afternoon, the unthinkable happened. Our boys were scheduled to play a football game against the Tipperary team at Croke Park. Although reluctant to do so, Annie and I let Jimmy go to the game with his best pal and his Da, my friend Daniel. It is too hard on a nine-year-old to give up on the pleasures of sport just because the world around him is going mad.

Typical of Irish festivities, the game got off to a late start. Then—and this was reported to me by Daniel—within about ten minutes the Black and Tan were shooting into the crowd from inside the turnstile entrances. Daniel took the two boys to the far side of the stadium and made them lie on the ground until the firing ceased.

It was sheer pandemonium. Panicked people fleeing the grounds were fired upon. Daniel stayed put with the lads, a wise decision. Before leaving, the security forces stopped him and told him he was to be searched. The guard, however, seeing the boys with their clothes tattered and crying uncontrollably, let Daniel pass quickly.

Jimmy was home by 6 p.m., still distraught. Annie gave him a warm bath, a light supper and spent the night in his room to assuage his nightmares.

The next day, the schools were closed. We went down to our parish hall where we found most of the other families had come for support. Daniel once again told his tale. We learned that one of our neighbor's daughters, a bonny lass named Jeannie Boyle, was killed. She was to be married later this week.

Two young lads from a neighboring parish were also shot down. All told, seven people were fatally wounded, including Michael Hogan, Jimmy's favorite footballer.

The Black and Tans have made our continuing relationship with the Crown unthinkable. There is increasing support for an end to all of this, but in my heart I know that will only come when Ireland is a nation on its own.

Keep us in your prayers, Maggie. My boy has witnessed man's inhumanity to man, a lesson he is too young to have learned.

With love and affection from your brother,

James

I started to shake when I finished reading James' words. I cannot imagine what it would feel like to have a child exposed to such senseless killing. I needed to talk with someone who would understand, and who could help me do the same. It was to Father Michael that I turned.

I was leaving after choir practice when I asked to see him. The air was chilled and he suggested that we go into the Rectory's parlor. As we sat down, I told him that I had just gotten the most horrific news from my brother and shared with him James's letter.

He shook his head slowly as he spoke, his eyes looking into mine.

Our land is going through terrible times, Maggie, he told me. *It is as if this Christian country that kept the faith alive for so many centuries, whose monks scribed the words of our Lord with such splendor that they are truly works of art, has lost its way.*

The hatred runs deep, and even the most fervent prayers of the most holy cannot seem to soften men's hearts. What your nephew witnessed in Dublin is played out in the streets of too many cities and towns. And there is blame on both sides.

As Jesus said: Let him who is without sin cast the first stone. If He gave that same challenge in the land I love so dear, no one would pick up a rock.

As he finished speaking, I saw that tears were falling softly from his eyes. It was all I could do to keep from taking him in my arms to console and ease his pain.

We shall continue to strive for peace, Maggie, and tell James that he and his wee lad will be in my prayers.

With that, he walked me to the door and we said our goodbyes. I watched as he walked away, taking a piece of my heart with him.

December

This year's Christmas Pageant was a great success. Sarah took the lead with the children so I could focus my attention on the choir. Father Michael and I were scheduled to end the evening's program by singing *O Holy Night*. As our allotted time approached, my nerves shot through me and I felt my throat go dry. Not at all like me.

Michael looked directly at me with those piercing blue eyes and nodded. He took the first poignant notes, firm, and strong. I returned his gaze, opened my mouth and, from a new reserve deep inside, sang as if this hymn belonged only to me, only to us. Our voices and our rhythms were as one, echoing in every crevice of the Church. It was a magical moment that took my breath away when it was over. You could have heard a pin drop.

Even Eli commented on how well we sang together.

Irish blood must still run through your veins, Margaret. You and Father Michael sounded like you have been singing together your whole life.

I drew a deep breath of the crisp, cold air and felt jubilant to be alive. A strange elation came over me; I felt like a falling snowflake being sent back to heaven by the force of a wind that called it as its own.

It is God's gift to me that Eli cannot read my thoughts, since Father Michael is occupying more and more of them.

January

We just returned from Belle's house where we had the most amazing experience. She has a radio, a large piece of furniture with numerous dials and a loudspeaker. We heard a broadcast of a baseball game that I couldn't care less about, but Eli was enthralled. He kept saying: *It's like I was right there. I can see it before my eyes!* He sounded like a child exclaiming over his Christmas stocking.

I was less impressed with the strikes, balls and misses repertoire than with the radio's sheer power to inform and to entertain. It can bring music into our homes, every night, from everywhere.

All were excited about this newest purchase except Eli's second cousin, Agnes. Never married, and always referred to as "Maiden Cousin Agnes," she put on her coat as soon as the radio was turned on. Adjusting her hat, she pronounced: *Radio is the handiwork of Satan. Voices from who knows where. Bodiless voices. It is not God's will to have people talk to you that you can't see and can't answer back. It is the end of the world. The final judgment will soon befall us all. I will not go into a house with voices coming in from nowhere.*

I think if Belle had known the radio would keep Agnes from visiting, she would have bought it years ago.

February

James writes of the most wonderful news.

I would love to talk with Michael and hear his views on what a free Ireland means to him, but that conversation happens only in my dreams. I close my eyes and see us seated quietly near the fireplace, its flickering light illuminating our faces while the sliver of the new moon peeks into the windows. I feel contented and engaged—body, soul and mind connected in unison.

I smile, recalling that image while I read James' message.

> My Dear Sister,
>
> It is done at last. We are a "Nation but One."
>
> As I am sure you have read in the American papers, a treaty has been signed ending British rule in 26 of our counties. By the end of this year, we will be a free state.
>
> It is not all as it should be, however. What the British named 'Northern Ireland'—and we call 'Ulster'—remains under British rule. I do not see how this can end well.
>
> The Catholics there, although a minority, want to join their brothers in the south, as they see themselves as Irish. The loyalists to the Crown are predominately Presbyterian, with a heritage that speaks more to Scotland than Ireland, or even England.
>
> I pray the day will come when we can live together as one, united by a land whose rolling hills, green fields and

bubbling brooks transcend the ranting and raving of the politics that consume us today.

I hope to be able to write no more of blood and senseless killings.

Annie and Jimmy are enjoying good health. We are looking at sending him away to school in two years' time. It will clearly break Annie's heart not to have him nearby, but it is in his long-term best interest. I am hoping he will be admitted to Clongowes Wood College, a Jesuit boarding school located near Clare in County Kildare with an excellent reputation. I believe it will do Jimmy well, though I, too, will miss him terribly.

With so many children of your own, it must be difficult to imagine what life with only one child is like. At times, it is hard to think that all your love and hope is tied into such a small person. But that is what it is.

With love and affection from your brother.

James

I came upon Michael in the choir loft, where he was picking at the keys and lowly singing a tune I never heard before. I was concerned that I was disturbing him, so made a ruffle with the sheets of music I had in my hand and was rewarded when he looked up at me. His eyes widened and I knew I had broken into wherever his mind was at that time.

Excuse me Father, I muttered, somewhat embarrassed to be broaching this private time.

No need to ever be excusing yourself, Maggie, he replied. a slow smile returning to his face as he stood away from the organ.

I heard from my brother that Ireland is now free. I thought you would be celebrating. James spoke of it as good news.

Michael shook his head slowly: *I fear the anger from those who are not in favor of this Anglo-Irish Treaty will continue to fuel the fire of conflict. There are those, and there are many of them, who believe that Michael Collins signing this agreement is not in the best interest of a free Ireland. There is going to be continued rebellion, only now it will be brother against brother.*

I didn't know what to say next, *I didn't recognize the tune you were playing*, was all I good think of.

He chuckled, deep and throaty; *you mean the tune I was picking at, Maggie. You know you must not lie to your parish priest*

The ballad was written by the curate at my church in Belfast, St. Peter's Cathedral. It tells the story of the Easter Uprising in Dublin, he called it the Foggy Dew. I remember most of the words and the melody.

And in as clear a voice as I ever heard him sing, he began

> *As down the glen one Easter morn*
> *To a city fair rode I*
> *There armed lines of marching men*
> *In squadrons passed me by*
> *No fife did hum, no battle drum*
> *Did sound its dred tattoo*
> *But the Angelus bells o'er the Liffey's swell*
> *Rang out through the foggy dew*

I then sat down at the organ, and said *let me try to follow you.*
He nodded and continued:

Right proudly high over Dublin town
They hung out the flag of war
'Twas better to die 'neath an Irish sky
Than at Suvla or Sud el Bar
And from the plains of Royal Meath
Strong men came hurrying through
While Brittania's huns with their long-range guns
Sailed in through the foggy dew.

As I picked up the melody and the accompaniment, Michael's
eyes and heart were somewhere else.

But the bravest fell, and the requiem bell
Rang mournfully and clear
For those who died that Eastertide
In the springing of the year
And the world did gaze in deep amaze
At those fearless men, but few
Who bore the fight that freedom's light
Might shine through the foggy dew.

He finished and sighed. *I pray that those that died that day will
not have done so in vain. And that the peace and freedom so
longed for will come without further blood staining our lands
and tainting our rivers.*

I looked up from my seat at the choir and said nothing. He
came over and gently squeezed my hand.

This helped Maggie. Thank you for being here for me. I will see you at choir practice tomorrow.

And then he was gone. I played the melody a bit longer, writing down the words as best I could remember. Though I understood Michael's sadness with the situation in Ireland, I couldn't contain my own happiness of spending this time with him, in this way. It was a moment to cherish. I hummed the *Foggy Dew* all the way home.

June

Michael is occupying more and more of my thoughts. I am quite foolish to even imagine him other than as my priest and my confessor. Yet I find myself looking forward to seeing him with a delight I have not ever felt. I must keep my emotions intact, though my imagination appears to take delight in conjuring up images of the two of us, walking in the fields, sipping tea, laughing at our private jokes. It is good that I keep these journals well hidden from any prying eyes. The words would condemn me in ways my actions never have.

September

I have often felt that the world is full of mystical powers we can't understand. It is good to know I am neither alone in that belief or in my sense of wonderment.

For so it is with James.

My Dear Maggie,

With all the troubles facing this Island, I fear I have not

made you remember how special our birthplace is, for it is a mystical land we are blest to call home.

Let me share with you a story from my youth—one that not even my beloved Annie has heard. And though I am a pragmatic man, a banker and a Catholic, I believe there are inexplicable forces, beyond our control and our imagination, that share our Ireland.

When I was not yet out of my teens, our uncle took me hunting out in the west. It was a cloudless day with no hint of a breeze. And yet, in an isolated spot about fifty yards from where we stood, a whirlwind appeared uprooting the grass and the heather. Our guide, a local man, strong and weather-beaten, put up his hand signaling us to stop.

In a voice only slightly louder than a whisper, but with the reverence of the altar boy ringing the bells at Mass, he said: 'Tis the fairies.'

Our party stood silent. The only sound to be heard was a strange buzz, a marching noise, as though the meadow had become a parade ground for these unseen crusaders. As this swirling wind moved toward us, we watched as if in a trance, unable and unwilling to move.

All at once, the wind surrounded us. Hands gripping our guns, trying to stay upright and resolute, and the hardiest of us attempting to smile bravely, we remained frozen. Our hair was blown about, and our caps flung into the fields.

Then, as quickly as it began, all went quiet. You could hear the stillness in the air. The fairies had passed.

Our party, young and old, men and boys who had not

been spared the burdens of living, were overcome with relief. Not a word was spoken, nor a glance exchanged. There was a lightness of spirit I have not felt before or after. Our guide merely nodded, commenting over his shoulder: "That's a sure sign of fine weather." And we were off. In true Celtic spirit, it was never spoken of again.

But you must believe me, Maggie, the fairies were there. I could feel them. I was bewitched by them.

It is a joy to be Irish.

With affection and love from your brother,

James

March

A hint of spring is in the air as an unexpected warm breeze makes its way into the barren garden. The sun belies that this is still winter as the weather is so fine it fills my heart with hope that warmer weather will arrive soon. Disappointment may come tomorrow with the reality of yet another snowfall, but for today, I reach out to the sun and it greets me back as a welcoming friend.

April

I am becoming increasingly agitated about needing to see Michael. It is like the addiction that some men have to alcohol—even when they know its dangers, they crave its intoxication.

May

Because I want to know more about Ireland, James writes to me of Dublin. I weave Michael into the pictures of this land that belongs to him and once was mine. I enter the world of 'what if', like a voyeur that creeps under his neighbor's snarled vines peering into his window, imagining the life being viewed as his own.

My Dear Maggie,

You have asked me to write about life in Dublin. It is a hard City to explain, perhaps because I am too close to see it as it really exists. It is home, and like an old friend I am comfortable with its flaws and shortcomings.

I will attempt to give you my view, then introduce you to one of my former school chums whose way with words is making him more famous each and every day. Yet I must warn you: he writes with a dark view of the world he grew up in, the world he has left behind.

Dublin is a complex place; it is small and compact so much has to be accommodated in this wee bit of land. We are a commercial center and, unlike your Buffalo, have never been known to focus on heavy industry. We do brew a good ale, however, and that has proven to make more than one family secure in their financial holdings. The rest of us are happy to contribute to their continued prosperity

Canals and roads essentially mark the city, and I watch with much stress as our key workers leave its center for towns and villages outside the square. Thus, the City is slowly becoming a population of badly housed and poorly fed people. Only the environs of Merrion Square, an area developed by English families' centuries before and where I currently reside, retains an air of higher status. But even here, the poor are never far away.

However, it is not a City of dirt and dust. Despite the impending decay, there is still an elegance to be found on our Georgian and Victorian streets. Ladies of fine quality, who shop in the morning and promenade leisurely in the afternoon, grace these walkways. My dear Annie has a few choice words to say about their like, but I am reluctant to share them with you. Trust me that she has more respect for the local charwomen than the peacocks strolling this path.

The River Liffey separates Dublin as we take to Grafton or Henry Street to do our shopping. Annie and I are the rare Dubliners who cross the Liffey to shop. Most of my colleagues are too posh to cross the O'Connell Bridge unless they are on their way to bet on a race in Phoenix Park or being carried, toes turned up, on their final journey to Glasnevin Cemetery.

To get another man's view of Dublin and Ireland, it is the author James Joyce I recommend to you. Joyce and I both attended University College, though years apart and of very different temperaments and world views. He studied languages and reserved his energies for extracurricular activities, reading widely, particularly books not recommended by our Jesuit teachers. The Dublin we knew then was a city of gaslights, horse-drawn carriages, outdoor plumbing and unpaved streets.

James' relationship with Dublin, Ireland, and the Catholic

Church became increasingly complex as the days passed. He left here for Paris over 15 years ago, amidst great controversy about his writing. I doubt he will return. His sister Eva followed him to France, but has since returned home. She sought me out at the bank upon her repatriation and we talked briefly about his decision to leave for reasons that were both deeply personal and reflective of broader societal trends.

Still, Eva shared my thinking that James will never be able to cut his ties to Dublin, even in Paris. She recounted that his favorite pastime is to seek out visitors from Dublin and ask them to repeat the names of the shops and pubs from Amiens Street to Nelson's Column on O'Connell.

I think both Dublin and Ireland tie you to them with bonds that cannot be broken, only strained.

With all that being said, I recommend you read James' *The Dubliners*. To put it in his own words: *I want to give a picture of Dublin so complete that if the city suddenly disappeared from the earth, it could be reconstructed out of my book.*

I think that is a bit of an exaggeration, not unlike Joyce's view of himself. However, with its reading you will get a sense of what life in Dublin is like; whether it is the interior of Mrs. Mooney's boarding house or Farrington's dark and troubled journey home. You will grasp the geography as experienced by his characters as they crisscross through my City's various streets. It is an incomplete picture, but I am sure it will engage you with the music of Dublin's language.

Your imagination will give you a sketch of Dublin, one I hope will whet your appetite to discover it more deeply. It is my greatest dream that someday I can personally show you this City I call home.

For now, I will let the infamous author James Joyce start that journey.

With love and affection,

Your brother,

James

The librarian was quite aghast when I asked for a copy of *The Dubliners*. In the hoarsest of whispers, as if she were in the confessional and I her priest, she whispered: *That book is sinful. It has been banned, and we would never have such a scandalous collection of short stories in our library. Are you sure you have the right title, Mrs. George? You seem like a Christian woman and all.*

I merely smiled and replied I must have gotten my titles mixed up as it was a book for one of the children's school projects. That seemed to satisfy her.

I left it to Belle to get the book for me. And she did, surprised that such a request would come from me. *I expect a complete book report, Margaret George,* she chided, handing it over.

I merely laughed and said that I likely wouldn't find time to read the book, let alone give her a summary. And with that, I took possession and planned never to speak of it again.

September

Leon refused to go hunting with Eli. He is all of 8 and Eli thought it was time he learned to shoot a gun.

Last month, he released the rabbits Eli had caught in the snare. Their shining black button eyes and soft fur reminded him of his childhood toys, and he could not bring himself to have them killed. No matter how Eli preached that they were varmints who ate our vegetables, Leon simply shrugged and walked away.

If I didn't know better, I might wonder if the two were even related, so different in temperament and outlook. They are like oil and water.

October

Michael came to dinner last night, entertaining the family with stories of Ireland and all its history. It was the first time my heritage has been a topic of conversation at our table and I would have been content to have him continue the tales for hours. Leon was enthralled and began to pepper him with questions.

Eli, however, grew impatient. When he finally spoke up, it was in a tone I have never heard him use to address a priest. With narrowed eyes, he broke into the conversation:

So, Father Michael, with all the talk of the beauty of Ireland and the warmth of its people, how could you find yourself leaving it to become a priest in America?

Michael was undaunted.

Well Eli, first you must understand that I came to the priesthood later in life than most. I fear that, like Augustine, I was called to the temptations of youth and greedily partook of them all. I was in my late twenties before I heard God call my name. Though it might not have been the first time, it was only then I was ready to listen.

After my ordination, our Bishop—who had just returned from a visit to the States—decided we should offer an exchange: one country priest in Ireland for one country priest in America. Since I had studied in London, they thought I was the logical candidate. And so here I am.

And all the better for it, I added, but only to myself.

The older children were intrigued—they had never heard a priest acknowledge he had been tempted, let alone sinned. Leon asked: *Who this "Augustine?"*

Michael threw his head back and laughed heartily, blue eyes smiling.

Describing Augustine requires more than a few brief sentences, my dear lad. Come see me later this week and I will introduce to you the man and the scholar. For he was both, and the Church and all its people are better for it.

With that, dinner was over. Eli wished him a good night and left to go back in the barn.

Later, I heard Louise ask her father about my being Irish. *Is that what makes her so different from us, Pa?* He scooped her up in his arms and whispered in her ear, just loud enough for me to hear: *Just one of the many things that makes your Mother so different from us, my little love.*

Yet even that exchange could not extinguish the glow of a lovely evening I just spent. Perhaps I am different than the rest but it is a good thing. Irish blood runs through my veins and it connects me with James and with Michael. That is enough.

December

My Dear Sister,

I send you the warmest greetings for this holiday. Despite the problems the world faces, we pause and celebrate the birth of the child who symbolizes peace and love.

To the extent we are able, Annie and I maintain the same Christmas rituals that were a mainstay in our childhood homes. Given the ravages of this last war, the goose will not be as plump or the cakes quite as moist as years past. Yet when I think of how many of our young lads have never returned to those they love, I can do nothing more than give thanks for our family.

Our Christmas Eve tradition—and I remember our Ma doing this is as well—is the "corneal more no Nolan," translated as "the big Christmas candle." Annie lights the candle at dark, and it safely burns in our kitchen window until the morning's light. We light it to show Mary and Joseph that, unlike the inn at Bethlehem, our house will always welcome them. Our doors are unlocked, and when we retire for the night, we leave food in three dishes upon the kitchen table as a welcome meal for these tired travelers.

In a time of too much strife and uncertainty, this simple gesture remains a warm and silent message of hope and welcome. In our house, in our city, and in cottages dotting our country lanes, we are sending slivers of light into the world. The clear December sky seems to reflect their glow in the stars that sparkle in the heavens. It is truly a silent, holy night.

May our children know a world of peace, my dear Sister. Lasting peace is the present we should give the world.

The happiest of Christmases to you, Eli and the children.

With love and affection,

Your brother,

James

I have a memory of Ma doing this, though it feels somewhat like a dream, rekindled by James' words.

In my reality, this Christmas Eve I will light a candle in the window and thank the Lord for the presence of James in my life. And, if I am brave, I will add Michael to that list.

On Christmas Day, it was not only the candles on the tree that burned bright day but Belle. She appeared at the door, hardly recognizable. Her beautiful, long hair has been bobbed and slicked down with a curl on each side of her face that covered her ears. Her skirt was short, her cheeks rouged, and she was wearing lipstick.

Eli was beside himself and told her he had never seen her look so ghastly. The young people, their friends and cousins in attendance, refuted his claim and told her she was "the bees' knees." Florence, now almost 6 years old picked up the chime, though she had no idea what it meant, and inspected Belle's legs to see if she could spot any hives.

As I looked closer, I realized Belle was no longer wearing a corset. When I questioned her after dinner, she confessed that all the whalebones in her closet had been tossed and she was a free woman in more ways than one.

There may be something about this flapper business that is in the best interest of all of us.

January

It has been months since Eli has sought me out in our marriage bed. I am not sure whether he has lost interest or is just too tired. For whatever his reason, it is fine with me. For I have begun to dream of Michael, so that I am both anxious before I fall asleep and reluctant to wake up in the morning.

I watch the rising sun touch the frost on my windows as it shatters the light into myriad colors. I remain still, eyes half-shut, reliving what I had dreamt, blushing, slightly breathless, and strangely content.

If this is a sin, who would I confess it to?

February

I look forward to James' letters. They brighten the darkest of days.

My Dear Maggie,

As I sit here, pen in hand and a whiskey poured, I have come to the thoughtful conclusion that your country's recent ban on alcohol, your Prohibition, could never be a law in this Island of our birth.

Mr. Guinness, world renowned for his stout, has enough political clout, both in this country and with the Crown, to ensure such nonsense would fail. This is the same Mr. Guinness, by the way, who will neither employ nor let his employees marry Catholics. He has no problem, however, selling us his brew and making his fortune doing so.

My university roommate has just returned from a business meeting in New York City. He felt quite at home at the Landmark Tavern, nestled on the shores of the Hudson River, likening it to his favorite local here in Dublin. Given your country's restrictions, the family has vacated part of its living space to entertain loyal patrons so they might quench their thirst without being taken in by the police. He was in their Speak Easy.

Now most don't know the term Speak Easy was coined by an Irishman. Or, to be more exact, an Irish woman.

According to legend, an elderly Irish widow made her living by selling illegal beer and whiskey to her neighbors and friends. A common practice in your country and not unheard of in this Kingdom as well. Having not been long gone from her native Roscommon, this seanbhean would warn her customers of a pending raid by exclaiming: *Spake asy, now the police are at the dure.* Hence, Spake Asy became the moniker for the hundreds of unlicensed taverns. In time, it Anglicized to Speak Easy, a term that universally describes such illicit liquor establishments for both its patrons and the raiding authorities.

In having a chat with the Landmark Tavern owners, my friend was told about a fellow cohort, a real chancer, who has parlayed his love of boats and booze to become a wealthy man, all thanks to your new laws. Willie McCoy left his job creating luxurious speedboats to become a rum-runner, bringing cases of genuine imported sprits to quench the thirsty. A very popular man, particularly for these owners and many of society's upper crust who have not lost their desire for the perfect Martini, he has faced unwelcome competition. The makers of moonshine and homemade concoctions trying to imitate his success claim their illicit drink to be "The Real McCoy." A simple tasting will confirm the falsehood of that propaganda.

It is true that the Irish have saved Western civilization from utter destruction by the Huns and the Germanic. We may also be rescuing America from the burden of the 18th Amendment.

May you continue to enjoy your cider. At least the government has not tried to stop you from delighting in the fruits of your orchard.

With love and affection,

Your brother,

James

March

I watched as the children from neighboring farms came home from school. Louise and her friends were chattering and giggling, their voices screeching with laughter as they skipped and stumbled along. Florence was leading the younger children in a game of tag, or some variation on that theme. I could not figure out the rules, but Florence was clearly in charge of whatever they were doing. She is always in the midst of the crowd, and is most alive when there are others around.

As usual, Leon walks alone, along the side of the road. It breaks my heart to see but there seems to be nothing I can so or do that breaks the wall he is building up around him.

They each are mine but so different.

April

It was not planned. I did not go to the church to see Michael. I did not know he would be in the church hall attic. At least that is what I tell my heart.

My task was to store the Easter decorations and take an inventory of what would be needed for the upcoming May Day procession. I had just finished climbing up the rope ladder to the attic when I heard him call my name. I jumped and, in doing so, stumbled on an uneven plank. He caught me in his arms to stop my fall.

I dared not look at him as he stood there, for my face would be evidence of what the sight of him did to me. I was so close, when I finally looked up, his eyes held my gaze.

And then he kissed me.

My body burned with desire and with longing. I opened up to him with my very being.

He dropped his face to the curve of my throat, nuzzling me, his mouth open against my skin. His hands were everywhere, touching me, pulling me tighter against him as he went on kissing me. I wanted to cry out for I was like a parched animal who had finally found the cistern of cold, clear water. I needed more. I needed to be quenched.

Amidst the boxes and wreaths, he gently drew me down to the floor, pulling my hair out of the tight roll at the nape of my neck while he kissed my mouth. His hands gently touched my face, my throat. His mouth then followed. His body became thick with purpose while mine softened, wet with longing. My flesh rose to him and then I could control it no longer. I had to become one with him. I pulled my dress overhead my head, as James undid any buttons and snaps that held me back from him.

I slid my hand into the open throat of his shirt to draw him down into a kiss deep enough to end all doubt. Kisses both light and demanding, then more demanding still, pulling off any piece of clothing. Then at last it was as it should be, all of my skin against his.

He ran a finger up my thigh and for the first time I called his name out loud. He gathered me up against himself.

Maggie, he whispered.

And then I burst, losing every sense of what was around me. I have never known such a sensation. I didn't know you could feel like this.

I became alive with a passion that I had never known before. I was burning as his tongue found me, I shuddered. His eyes raised and found mine as he slowed down the pace, gently caressing every part of me, until I cried out for more. I pushed myself into him with all my might. He stayed within me as we rocked and held on to each other as if the Apocalypse were dawning.

When it was over, he smoothed my hair and cradled me in his arms. I moved closer to him. He whispered: *We have sinned. But for this moment, just hold me. Please.*

I could feel his chest against my cheek and the weight of his arms around my shoulders. We lay there, knowing what we had done. I was satisfied and content. Any regret that might come later, would be for what I have missed, not for what I had done. I now understood the pleasure and joy of giving all I was capable of giving and having that same gift returned.

Eventually, we gathered up our things, our backs to each other as we dressed. Time had stood still for me, and yet a lifetime had passed since I entered the storage attic.

He took my hand in his and led me down from the stairs. As we came to the door, he gently spoke: *Maggie, we need to talk of this, but not today. Go home. I will come to you there.*

And I did.

I know it was wrong and I have committed a mortal sin. But it all felt so right at the moment. I don't know what I will do, but I cannot say I am sorry.

If only for a moment, I felt loved and cherished. I am not sure how I can continue living as I have, to go back to life that was mine just hours ago. I now know what I have missed. I now know what I will never have.

For one of the few times in my life, I dare not think about tomorrow. I can only try to make it through today.

Days Later

I have not been to church or choir practice this week. I cited an illness that I know has no physical origins. I cannot bear the thought of seeing Michael—it would be too much, and I am not sure I could pretend that life is the same as it was prior to our being together.

Eli accepted my behavior as just one more of my female dispositions. And since it is planting time, thankfully, he is engrossed in the farm and the livestock. I am left alone with my thoughts and my increasing sense concern of what will happen next.

May

The garden is the only place I can find peace as the scent of lilacs drifts around me. Bees humming and robins chirping in the maples are the only sounds that bring me comfort.

It was here, in my sanctuary, that I heard my name called. I looked up. The sun was blazing through a gap at the top of the hill, blinding me. Against it, there he stood, like a messenger from the Almighty, a force in the distance looming over me.

I brushed the hair from my face as he came towards me.

Michael, I mumbled.

I have missed you, Maggie. I will always miss you. And you must know that I am leaving Sheldon at the end of June. My bishop has written that there is much trouble in Ireland, particularly in Belfast, with gangs on both sides of the political strife committing atrocities beyond our imagination. Innocent and not so innocent people are being murdered, some in their own homes. There are those who think I may be of use in trying to find some path to peace. I am not sure how much good I might do, but my orders are to leave as soon as possible. It is probably for the best.

I started to shake. Michael took my hand.

We have sinned, Maggie. Yet we know our place in this world. You are a wonderful mother, and a companion and wife to Eli. I am a priest. I have answered God's calling, and no matter how strong my feelings for you are, my love for you cannot turn me away from the path I have chosen.

We must accept the lives that we have set for ourselves that I believe God has set for us. And today, I come to you as your priest, to give you absolution as you confess your sins.

I looked into his eyes, as blue as the sky that engulfed us. In a small voice, I began, *Bless me Father, for I have sinned.*

I cannot remember anything else I said until Michael placed his hand in mine: *Let us pray to our Mother Mary in the language of our grans and our grans before them:*

Se do bhava, So do breathe, a Mhuire, atá lán de ghrásta, Tá an Tiarna leat. Is eannaithe thú idir mná, Agus is beannaithe toradh do bhroinne, Íosa. A Naomh-Mhuire, a Mháthair

Dé,guigh orainn na peacaigh, anois, agus ar uair ár mbáis.
Amen.

I stumbled at first; it had been too many years since I spoke the Old Language. But I finished strong, the Amen resounding throughout the quiet grounds where we were now kneeling.

Quietly, I heard the words: *Your sins are forgiven.*

We stood. Michael brushed his lips to my hair: *At the hour of my death, Maggie, when I am ready to meet the Lord, it will be your face that I see.*

And then he was gone.

Tears came, for the first time since Nell had left me and I fell to the ground. After I cried myself out completely, I felt calmer.

A strange, icy numbness descended upon me. I slowly stood up, the imprints from my knees still impressed upon the grassy mound.

The afternoon sun lingered in the air, silencing the farm with a wordless hush. I marveled that the apple trees could retain their pink blossoms, that the grass could still grow, the birds still sing. My world had changed completely, yet all around me had stayed the same.

As I made my way out of the garden, I found a baby bird that had fallen from its nest—no doubt in its first attempt to escape the confines of the twigs and dried leaves it called home. I made sure that there was no life left, fell on my knees, and dug a hole deep enough to keep its still body safe from the squirrels and scavengers that stalk these hills.

As I stood over my makeshift grave, I thought of another time, long ago, when I had been living in Sheldon about a year or two. I was taking a shortcut home from school when I found what I thought to be a dead bird.

I scooped it up in my hand and brought it home, planning to give it a first-class burial. Father found me, looked at the bird in my cupped hands and told me to lay it quietly on the ground. As I stared at the mass of feathers, one of its eyes slowly opened and looked back at me.

Father gently beckoned me to join him on the front porch, motioning me not to say a word. There we sat watching as the bird, a bright red cardinal, righted himself, hopped around, and after giving us a very brief nod took flight.

Father looked at me: *Sometimes Margaret, things are not as we first think them to be. Do not rush to act. Like our bird, even when the unexpected happens, we may only need time until we are back on the path that God and nature have planned for us.*

I don't know why that memory is so vivid today. I haven't thought of it, or Father, in such a very long time.

I wonder which bird is Maggie Clancy—the one whose life was cut short by too early an attempt to escape, or the one that simply needed a bit of time to test its wings and strength before taking flight.

June

After being gone close to a month, it took all my strength to return to church and this evening's choir practice, but I had no choice. Michael is preparing to leave, and the ladies are all abuzz about the send-off they are planning. No one seemed fazed that I was quiet and not offering to take a lead role in the event.

As the days pass, I question whether I might crumble from the sheer weight of emptiness engulfing me. I had Sarah lead the practice, as I was shaking inside, fearful that I might collapse, afraid of breaking my silent vow to keep it all hidden away from the outside world.

And as the organ's vibrations filled the choir loft, my prayers were answered. I exorcised those pent-up feelings by lifting my voice into song. I sang with the suppressed passion and sadness that haunt my day-to-day existence.

When the practice was finished, I knew I had the courage and resolve to make it through the farewell celebrations being held in Michael's honor.

This Sunday was Michael's last Mass. The day dawned bright and clear, in contrast to my mood. I walked the steps leading up to the church doors, and slowly the emotions that had been so raw and sharp began to ebb. The bulbs that had been planted on a cold, dark autumn afternoon were now in full bloom. Tulips in myriad colors graced the path, with rolling green hills serving as their backdrop. The beauty and majesty of this countryside was breathtaking. God has a plan for all things, and that includes me. As I stopped at the open door to dip my fingers into the holy water font, I made a silent prayer to be granted the strength to make it through this day.

Slowly, I ascended the steps to the choir loft in what felt like a hazy dream. I calmly took my place at the organ, my familiar spot as head of the choir, and acknowledged the nods of those already present. Once again, music was my refuge and my silent prayer answered. I reached into pile of music sheets and pulled out the *Ave Maria*. Before my fingers touched the keys of the organ, I hummed the first note. The choir followed suit, our voices linked.

As our voices faded into silence, I turned and looked down at the altar to see Michael smiling up at me. My cheeks were wet with tears that had silently fallen. He brushed a tear away as our eyes met. We had said our last farewell. No words were needed.

As I moved to the next selection, I gave up my seat at the organ to Sarah, and an unexpected peace came over me. I knew I was in the place I needed to be. The place I needed to stay.

July

I am pregnant.

I know well enough the feeling. And it is Michael's child.

I will be sure Eli will never doubt its paternity. He and I will come together as man and wife tonight.

1923-1933

M ore than 10 years have passed since I held this
journal in my hands. The Margaret that penned
these pages is but a faint memory.

So much has happened, and so much has stayed the same. I
am ready to begin again, although my handwriting has
become more of a scribble than the fine example of
penmanship expected of the Senior Girl. Perhaps it is God's
way to ensure this journal's secrets stay mine alone. Or
perhaps it is that my mind leaps forward too quickly and my
hand cannot capture my thoughts fast enough.

Those first few months after Michael left, I felt as though I
were watching myself go through the motions of living. My
sense of loss was everywhere: overwhelming, inexorable,
deafening. I wasn't myself, but only someone watching me
being me, a shell of the woman I once was. Slowly, I learned
to carry on, to fill the void as best I could, rather than
disappear into it. Yet somewhere in the emptiness of that

shell, a seed began to grow and the woman I am today took flower.

Catherine

Throughout my pregnancy with Catherine, I lived in fear that, once born, everyone would recognize the child as Michael's. Yet after she entered this world, it seems I was the only one to realize that those clear blue eyes do not belong to her alone.

Belle may have her suspicions as she remarked on Catherine's first birthday that she looked quite different from the rest of the family. I merely smiled and replied: *Perhaps it is her Irish heritage. After all, Florence has somehow gotten my eyes.*

Not even Belle can know that truth, and Eli has never suspected.

During these dark days, it was Catherine who kept my sanity intact. Whenever I saw her, she bubbled with joy, reaching out to be held in my arms. The other children essentially ignored her, except Florence. From the moment she was first introduced, Florence decided Catherine was her special gift and hers alone. The two became as one, Catherine's first word was a heartfelt *'Rence,* the name she calls her sister to this day.

Today, Catherine is a unique child. Her smile is a benediction; her joy in the simple pleasures of life runs deeper than what you would expect from a child her age.

I love my children; they tether me to the wheel of life. But it is Catherine, the offspring of love rather than duty, who lightens my heart.

Leon and Walter

Eli doesn't know what to make of his two boys. My husband craves the order and routine of his own childhood, when his father told him and his brothers what to do. If they disobeyed or got out of line, they got a whipping to help them remember the next time. And should the possibility of a next time occur, the memory of the beating would deter its repetition. He and his brothers became boys who worked hard with only a nod from their father when a job was well done.

It is not like that with either Leon or Walter. Leon cares nothing for the land and makes no pretense about it. At 16 he left school and two years later continues to work in a Buffalo steel factory during the week, coming home on the occasional weekend. He has grown to become the mirror image of his father. When I see him, I see the Eli I married: broad in the shoulders with hands and feet that were bred to work the fields. But his head is somewhere else, though it is not clear where. He cares for neither books nor the barn. A loner by nature, he keeps his own solace and often seems to be onlooker rather than a participant in the world around him. Yet, he is my first-born and I ache for him to be happy, or at least at peace. He and his father have dissolved into a relationship that allows for nothing more than a quick word now and then. Should the conversation last longer than a minute, it becomes a shouting match that scares the other children and petrifies me.

Walter has the look that must come somewhere from my side, though Eli would never admit as much. He is tall and slender with wavy dark hair and eyelashes the girls all crave. He has a natural way with people and that ease translates to how he handles all living creatures, including the animals. It is he who is up with Eli to tend to the cows. It is Walter that understands what earth needs to rest and where the corn should be planted. Eli is patient with him, explaining things in a way he never could or never did with Leon.

But despite his aptitude, Walter doesn't have the temperament to be a farmer. He has little tolerance for routine, and the constant demands of this life agitate him. He cannot charm the cows to wait another day to be milked or talk the hay into bundling itself. He pleases his father only because he abhors conflict. He would rather turn the other cheek than to strike. He does not wish to be in the same place as his older brother.

Louise

When she was ten, Louise looked fourteen and acted eighteen. She was a child that wanted to be an adult before she was ready, and that was the choice she made, apparently without regret, at least so far.

Shortly after her 16th birthday, she decided to leave school but had no plans as to what she was going to do. We see the world through a different lens. Although our relationship had not deteriorated the way Eli and Leon's had, we could find no common ground on which to agree.

She told me once that she never understood what all the fuss was about in giving the women the vote. *I am perfectly happy let the men decide all those things,* she told me. *I don't care a lick for what some politician does in Washington, DC, or even in Albany. Let someone else worry about that. It's all those women voting that got prohibition passed, destroying any fun I might have.*

I started to point out the reasons why women needed the vote. I was in the middle of my lecture, when she got up from the table and looked at me with the greatest of disdain. *I simply don't get you and Aunt Belle. Why not leave well enough alone? You're always poking your nose into things that aren't yours to care about.*

I want to be a wife and mother, and be there for my husband and children. Because you never were, Mother. There was always something more important for you to do or take care of other than Pa and us kids. We saw Sarah more than we saw you. Well, that won't be the case with me and my kids. I will always be there for them, and happy to do so.

Eli walked in just as Louise was finishing her diatribe. *That's my little girl,* he said, putting his arm around her. *Some lucky man will be happy to be at your side at the altar. Just don't make that too soon. I am not ready to lose you.*

Oh Pa, she swooned back. *You will never lose me. I'll be your daughter forever and one day more.*

They both looked at me. I saw them united in a cause, and that cause was to attack me. I had no recourse, but Louise's accusations struck home. She had hurt me in my most vulnerable spot. And she knew it.

It was early spring the night she didn't come home. She had gone on a picnic with Frank Victor and a group of friends, or so she told us. I didn't notice that a bag had been packed and hidden under the bushes by the driveway as I later learned. I woke up at midnight and found no sign of her at home.

I shook Eli awake. *Louise isn't t home.* I started to tremble, *do you think there was an accident?* My mind flashed with pictures of broken limbs, blood on the hood of the car, bodies thrown into the fields. The phone rang before he could answer me. He picked it up and I only heard his voice.

Are you all right? Your Mother and I are . . . You're what? When? You need to get home tonight, do you understand? I will not have this, Louise. You are a child. Get home now. He stared at the phone, blood draining from his face.

I pulled the belt on my robe tighter as I went to him. His face had changed colors; now it was red with rage. *What happened? Is she okay? What about the others?*

There are no others, he snarled. *Only Frank. They got married in Niagara Falls. They're at a hotel somewhere in Canada.* I felt like I might faint. This couldn't be happening. *Impossible,* I moaned, *she is only a child.* Eli pulled me into a chair as I started to fall.

He went on: *I only know that Louise had it all arranged. She said she contacted a local justice of the peace, got all the paperwork completed, and hid her bag. They were married this evening.*

But she barely knows him, I said. *They have only been dating a few times. Or that was what she claimed.* I started to clear my head. All those times, she was leaving to see her friends, was it really Frank she was going to see? I had not done my duty by her. I had not protected her. And now she was out of my reach.

Eli was quiet, his eyes hollow. *We can do nothing tonight. She was clear she wasn't coming home and we would see her and her husband tomorrow,* he said sadly. *I wasn't even able to walk my little girl down the aisle.*

His voice now stronger, more in command, he continued *I will go to the Victors in the morning and work out the details. I will also stop by the rectory and let Father know what has happened, so they can be properly married in the church where she was baptized.*

I simply nodded and slunk lower into my chair. He came over, knelt beside me and took my hand. *It will be all right, Margaret. It is what Louise has always wanted: a home and husband of her own. The Victors are good people and we will come to know Frank.*

But she is just a girl, I stuttered. *A girl with her own mind,* he responded. *And I know where she gets that from,* he smiled. I smiled back and took his other hand. *Let us just be sure we have her properly married as soon as possible. And no fanfare, please. Just the two of them, with the Victors and us as witnesses.* He took my hand to his lips, *you have my word, Margaret. No fanfare.*

And he kept his promise. Within two days, Louise was back home, married by a priest and had moved in with her new in-laws. Within six months, she and Frank had their own home and a baby on the way. I didn't want to count the months when my grandson was born. It simply didn't matter.

Eli seems to have forgotten all the circumstances leading up to his namesake being born. Now Louise, Frank, baby Eli, and another baby whose birth is imminent are a two-mile walk over the meadow. Eli visits regularly. I, on the other hand, find my visits uncomfortable for both Louise and me.

So, I keep my distance, which emotionally is more than two miles.

Florence

And then there is Florence. Intelligent, quick-witted and, occasionally, strong-willed. Thanks to her natural enthusiasm to relish life at every turn, she is popular with both teachers and classmates. While she shares my thirst to know more about everything, her looks resemble Nell, or at least what I think Nell might have looked like at the same age. I smile when I think that she is the blend of the two of us.

Following Louise's elopement, I started hovering over Florence, questioning where she was going, who she was going with, and checking on her every movement. I was not going to make the same mistake twice. Florence would have none of it. She was almost fifteen, but with a mind of own, a trait that I seem to pass on to all my girls.

She found me in the garden one afternoon, and with a voice more confident than her years should allow, told me we had to talk. The day was bright, the sun unforgiving, so I suggested we find a spot in the shade. Before I had even found a comfortable spot under the welcoming maples, Florence took a deep breath and began. It was clear that she was to do the talking. I was only to listen.

I am not Louise, Mother, and you know that. I want to do things with my life. To see more of the world, to see what Aunt Belle has seen. I don't how I am going to do that, but I have plenty of time to figure that out. You don't need to be a hawk where I am concerned. And that goes for Catherine as well. Both of us love school, and want to learn more. You know that was never true of Louise.

I don't want my education to end in Sheldon. When the time comes, we will need to figure out how I will finish high school. For now, please trust me that I will do what is right.

I smiled. This was my daughter all right, but with a maturity and insight I did not have at the same age. I may have failed Louise, but I had not done so with Florence. Nor with Catherine. At least not yet.

I took her hands and stared into those eyes so like my own. *You have my word. I love you.* With a smile, she replied, *I love you, too, Mother.* We got up from our garden spot, and with a quick kiss on my cheek and a wave of her hand, she was off. I don't know to where, but I needed to trust her, a trust she has not broken to this day.

That night after supper, I mentioned to Eli that Florence may be interested in getting her high school diploma, an achievement to which neither her brothers nor Louise ever aspired. *Sheer foolishness,* was his reply. *Why go to all that trouble just to stay at home and have babies? Louise is doing it just right. Besides, she needs to be under our roof until she has a husband and a home of her own. She is not to be living somewhere on her own, out of our sight.*

I didn't have the strength to argue.

There would be time enough down the road for me to make the case.

Yet in typical Florence fashion, she took the decision as to whether she should attend high school right out of our hands.

It was about six months after our garden discussion, and Florence had just turned 15. Eli had gone over to see Louise and the baby, deciding to walk since the day was so bright and warm. I was working on the books for the Ladies of the Hill when I saw the car pull out into the road with Florence behind the wheel. Leon had taught her how to drive, but to the best of my knowledge, she had never been in the car alone. I rushed out to the porch to see her start up the hill without so much as a backward glance.

Later that evening, Eli and were at the kitchen table going over my latest entries in the farm ledger when she pulled back in the driveway, smiling like the cat that had finished a bowl of cream. Eli started with: *Who gave you permission to take the car?* Florence never flinched as she replied*: No one. But I have such news.* And with that, she preceded to tell us that she had driven to the high school in East Aurora and met with the principal. She had a letter of introduction from Miss Bechtel, her current teacher who graduated from there.

Our mouths dropped in amazement.

Well, my darling daughter had worked out an arrangement with the principal that she could complete her high school diploma by studying at home. Miss Bechtel, whose family still lived in East Aurora where she returned each weekend, would bring the assignments to her each Monday and Florence was to complete them by the end of the week. Miss Bechtel would then return them to someone at the high school and the process would repeat.

Florence had found the compromise that neither Eli nor I would have proposed. She would not live away from home, so

Eli was pleased. And, as for my wishes, she could continue her education.

Florence smiled sweetly at her father. *I put a dollar's worth of gas in the car, Pa.* He sputtered a bit as he added, *And I expect you to wash it, inside and out.* With a nod of agreement and a sweep of her skirt, she was off.

Thank the Lord you're back safe, was all I could think. But my joy could not be contained. I thought of Mr. Altimeter and how hard it was for me to get permission to become a teacher. My Florence took matters into her own hands and was carving out her own future. I couldn't be happier for her or for me.

James

James kept me amused and informed. His letters were a respite, a glimpse into another world. I could close my eyes and picture us chatting about the issues he was raising or the advice he was offering. I would make myself a cup of tea, and as I read them I heard his voice.

Dear Maggie,

I continue to marvel at how mismanaged and misguided those who have so much sway over our lives seem to be. Our economy is in disarray, Dublin is overcrowded, our working classes suffer from poor health, and our young people are fleeing to other lands to find their future. The wounds of our bitter civil war have not yet healed. Yet amidst all this heartache and uncertainty, our government and church leaders are focusing on unsupervised dancing among our young people as their biggest concern for the country. I cannot make this up, my sister, and if I didn't take my baptismal vows so seriously, I might look to find another path to lead me to Jesus.

Two years after our women were given the right to vote, our bishops in their Lenten addresses sought to list women's fashion among the many abuses their faithful were committing. Now, I am not a man that fails to notice a lovely colleen, but these words were being preached by those who have taken a vow of celibacy. It would seem to me much easier to keep that promise if less time was spent ogling the opposite sex's supposedly immodest attire. But other horrors such as indecent dancing, theatrical performances, and the cinema also made the list. Queen Victoria may be dead, but the morality code she espoused predominates our culture today, even here in Ireland.

The root culprit, the source of all these modern-day evils, is none other than the poor motor car. Thanks to your Mr. Ford, our young people have too much mobility and can now travel great distances to dance. The horror is our simple country parish dances can now be attended by unsuitables. Although not defined, we can safely assume that the bishops' esteemed fingers are pointed at boys from the city.

Jimmy has his own car, and Annie and I have placed strict rules as to where he can go and with whom. For I do not think either the Church or the government should replace parents as the moral compass for their children. Perhaps it makes sense to limit the days and hours that dance halls may operate, but let us not blame the poor motor car as the source of wickedness.

My heart aches when I ask the authorities to describe their plan on how to address the pressing issues facing this land of ours: poverty, unemployment, the expatriation of our youth. But like John the Baptist, I fear that I, too, am the voice crying out in the wilderness. And the wilderness hears it not.

With love and affection,

Your brother.

James

The Ladies of the Hill

It is funny when I now look back and see how this all began. Not funny as if it were a joke, but the irony of how the fates once again conspired to change my life. It was 1928 and my world would never be the same again.

It was a normal market day, and I was in East Aurora peddling my goods when I happened upon Sarah selling her eggs. At lunchtime, we took our baskets and found shelter from the blazing sun, the air so thick you could cut it with a butter knife, to find refuge under the large elm in the park.

Sarah looked so tired. I remember her on her wedding day; the little girl I taught to play the piano was a beautiful bride. Now, her hair that had once shone with the joy and promise of the future lay flat and unkempt.

Confusingly, she said she didn't know what she was going to do. Then she started to cry, not the sobs of an aching heart or a hurt that needs to heal. Rather, these were the slow and salty tears of despair trickling down that face once so fresh and full of life.

Regaining her composure, she explained her struggle to keep up the work involved with the market produce. Her older children were beginning to help with feeding the chickens and egg gathering, but it was still left to her to do the crating and the selling.

Sarah's shoulders slumped: *With the washing and cooking for the two older children, and keeping the baby nursed and bathed, I barely have time to feed myself let alone watching out for the hens. And we need the money. It is the only cash money we really have and Thomas counts on it. He never says so exactly. You know how our men are. They would never say they rely on us to help with the farm. That is their job. To them, this is just a sideline.*

Then, she looked up and her brown eyes flashed with a trace of her old spirit: *A sideline. A sideline that supports our family with no help from him. I am so tired there are days I simply don't know if I can carry on one more moment. Being in the church choir was such a pleasure, and I don't even have the time and energy to do that anymore. It is just so hard.*

With that, she wiped her face, picked up her basket, and left. My heart broke remembering the little girl who had bartered helping with my babies to learn how to play the piano. How unhappy she was today. I wished there was something I could do to help ease her the pain I recognized so well.

There and then is where the idea began to form. As I drove

back to the farm, I wondered what could happen if the women pooled their eggs and chickens and worked together as one to sell them at the market. Just like the men were doing with their milk.

We knew the model for the cooperative already and understood how it worked. We could share the chores and potentially increase our profits. No longer would we have to individually haggle over prices at the market. We could be more productive and more profitable.

It was Belle, true to form, who put the idea into action. We were in a restaurant in Buffalo, celebrating my upcoming birthday, when I shared my thinking. She was ecstatic about the idea of a woman's cooperative. *Best idea you ever had, Margaret. Second only to becoming friends with me. So, now let's think of what it means.*

First, you need a name. Since you all farm on or near Buffalo Hill, we shall simply call you The Ladies from the Hill. It is simple, classy, and not confining. You don't want to be called hen and eggs ladies because who knows what else you may want to include.

I laughed out loud. Only Belle would have us moving beyond our scope before we had even started, in fact before we had even become a "we." I did, however, like the name: "The Ladies from the Hill." I nodded my agreement.

Her next question: *Who are you expecting to join?*

Well, I had given this some thought. *I have four women, members of the choir, that I think could serve as a core group. They each have a specific set of talents that either complement or contrast with mine.*

I went on, thinking out loud as the ideas began to crystallize. *The entire group should be no more than eight, so we would add three more. My thinking is that all need to meet three criteria: first, they already had to have a chicken-and-egg business, so they understand what goes into maintaining and selling our goods; second, they have to be selling in one of the markets: either East Aurora or Batavia, as we initially need entry into those marketplaces; and third, while not critical, it would be helpful if their husbands were already participating in the dairy cooperative. That way, they have an understanding of how it works.*

As I laid it in front of Belle, she began to nod. *You always were the smart one, Margaret. My sense is you are right in keeping the group fairly limited at this initial stage. But let's get other thinking on this.*

And with that, Belle got up and asked the maître d' to use the phone.

Minutes later, my hair flying out of my hat, she was hailing a cab, and we were on our way to her lawyer's office.

You're putting the cart before the horse, Belle, I stammered. *I have not even talked to anyone else about this idea. I have never talked to a lawyer before. I don't even know what I can say.*

Belle replied: *Hogwash. You are not going to do anything until you get some legal advice. You need to protect yourself and your business from competing interests, and that includes those of my dear brother, Eli.*

I nodded my agreement, surprised by her sentiments yet somehow knowing she was right. And that was that.

The law office Belle ushered me into was intimidating, an effect I assumed to be intentional.

We entered a reception area; its chandelier dangling crystals drops that shone like diamonds upon wood polished so brightly you could use it as a mirror. A young woman dwarfed behind a desk rose and escorted us into a conference room, larger than my kitchen and parlor combined.

It was all I could do to contain myself from running my hands over the rich brocade tapestry of the curtains. I took my cues from Belle, who seemed quite at ease in this den of finery, and nodded my agreement that tea would not be necessary.

Minutes later, Belle's attorney arrived, looking exactly like an attorney should. Mr. Schrader was tall, with a crisp white shirt and pressed dark blue suit with a watch nestled comfortably in its vest pocket. The only wrinkles that would ever dare make their way near him were the laugh lines around his sharp brown eyes that belied the pompous bearing he cultivated.

I thought about James' comment that sometimes it is the packaging that counts. I was not disappointed that this gentleman could be my lawyer.

As the discussion began, Belle was her most charming. She clearly knew he would be pleased to see her, despite the last-minute interruption to his day. After initial pleasantries, she got down to business. This was a Belle I did not know.

She synthesized my idea, emphasizing how this vision would not have even been possible until women got the vote. She told Mr. Schrader she wanted to be sure I had a clear understanding of the business parameters and financial obligations I was about to undertake.

Mr. Schrader nodded thoughtfully, asked questions, took notes, and then put his pen down.

Makes perfect sense to me, Mrs. George. I am not familiar with the legal structure of co-operatives, but I have some colleagues who have done work in that area. Let me check with them.

I also think we should look to setting up a banking account, so that you keep the finances of the co-operative separate from your individual home accounts. We can make the books open to all members of the co-operative to review at any time. Belle, I think your banker, Joseph Harrison would be just the right person to help set that up.

Let me take this under advisement. Should we plan to meet in the next week or two and see what progress we have each made? Mrs. George, I will leave it up to you to organize The Ladies from the Hill. Leave the behind-the-scenes to me.

Before I knew it, we were walking out into the late afternoon.

I was in a state of shock. I had come to Buffalo with an idea to share with Belle and left with my own attorney and a potential banker. I had no idea how I was going to mention this to Eli.

Belle, however, was ebullient. *Come, Margaret. Time for champagne to celebrate your new venture. This is simply wonderful.*

I wasn't quite sure it was wonderful. I did know I could use a drink.

That night, I wrote to James about my idea for "The Ladies from the Hill." It was helpful to be able to get my thoughts in order, and the plan began to take shape as I started to write.

The irony did not escape me that I was first sharing my ideas with a lawyer I had never met and an Irish banker miles across the sea before I talked it through with my own husband, a man who has been a farmer all his life and ran a cooperative.

Two weeks later, Belle once again stirred the pot. I had come into town to meet with Mr. Schrader and was spending the night with Stella and her. Eli was getting more and more accustomed to my being away from home for a night or two and didn't seem to mind too much.

Belle was once again hosting one of her soirees, and I became engaged in a lively discussion with one of her new friends, Sheila, a nurse working at the Sisters of Charity Hospital in the Pharmacy Department. Sheila has the look of a person you could trust, with a sense of self that brings the words "reliable" and "sensible" to mind. Her manner of dress is neither old-fashioned nor stylish—it could have been bought yesterday or years ago. But her no-nonsense demeanor belied her passion about the need for patients to have fresh food that the hospital staff could rely on. *The meals we provide our patients should help them heal rather than slowly poison them.*

I told her that I sell fresh eggs and chickens once a week at the local market in East Aurora, and how it was important to gain the trust of our buyers by the quality of the products we were selling. She, unlike Eli's farmer friends, was interested in my record keeping—I knew what hens laid the best eggs and what cows produced the most milk. She was truly excited when I explained my records could tell what animals were the healthiest and which ones were in difficulty. *Not unlike our patient record-keeping*, she observed.

Belle put herself front and center in the conversation and boasted I was about to start a cooperative to sell fresh eggs and chickens in the marketplaces. To my surprise, she told Sheila that the hospital should buy its eggs from *The Ladies from the Hill*. Everyone would be a winner: the hospital would get a reliable source for its eggs, the patients would get fresh food, and Sheila would be helping a group of fledgling women business owners get started.

Sheila nodded and asked if I could produce four cases of eggs of week. I did a quick calculation. That was 120 dozen eggs, an enormous amount, and I didn't have enough hens on my farm to meet that demand.

But, for whatever reason—today I still don't know why—I said I could do it. Sheila was enthusiastic and said she would write out the particulars after she talked to the Head of Pharmacy, who was responsible for the patients' nutritional needs.

The following week, after choir practice, I asked four of the women to stay behind. I began by describing my meeting with Sheila, doing my best to explain what had transpired, and outlining the pluses and minuses of the enterprise I was proposing. My last meeting with Mr. Schrader had given me the particulars I needed to discuss the risks and reward we might incur in this potential venture.

We can be friends, and we can share a common interest in making ourselves secure in our finances. I calculated that we can supply Sisters of Charity their eggs and keep our market folks satisfied, if we pool and add to our flocks. If the men can do it with milk, we can surely do it with our eggs and chickens.

As I looked at the women assembled, I wondered what I had gotten myself into. This core group of farmers' wives bore little resemblance to leaders of an upstart business that required the likes of upscale legal and financial counseling.

Even now, when I close my eyes, I can see them around me in a semi-circle. First, there was Rita, with the pink cheeks and blue eyes of long-faded prettiness. She has an air about her of a rare and genuine innocence, in the most literal meaning of the word, that makes it impossible to take offense, however personal her questions and comments. She is well-liked among the other women both at church and in the marketplace. I knew she would be a good alter ego to my more formidable self.

Next to her was Eva, whose waistline is ever-increasing. Yet it is her twinkling eyes and a face made for laughter and enjoying life that draw you to her. She always looks as if she is about to burst forth with some great joke. From the beginning, Eva would keep the group intact with her good nature and easy personality.

Across from me was Elizabeth. Ginger-haired and ever alert, Elizabeth's mind is sharp as a tack, with the ability to find solutions when others are not able to identify the issues. I knew that without her involvement, our chances for success were limited.

And then there is Mary, broad-faced with shoulders to match. She can taste dirt and tell you what is needed to make your flowers grow brighter and your vegetables take root. With animals, big and small, she has a way that cannot be taught by the grange experts. If we were looking to draw a picture of Mother Nature, Mary would be our model.

These farmers' wives, mothers of broods of children, who have never left Western New York, would become the core group of what has turned out to be the most amazing adventure for all of us. But at that moment, I held my breath as I finished my last statement. Eyes open and mouth shut, I waited until one or all of them would begin to speak.

To my delight, each, true to their nature, was totally committed from the start. Elizabeth was able to do the calculation and saw the opportunity to make more money by pooling our joint efforts. She was in.

Rita asked if I was putting myself in place to lead the group, and I confirmed I was. Eva simply threw her head back and laughed: *This will be great fun. Our husbands will be beside themselves.*

I proposed our name: "The Ladies from the Hill."

Mary roared: *I love it. Though I never thought of myself as a lady when I was behind the plow.*

And thus, it all began. *The Ladies from the Hill,* it was. Simply, directly, and with no idea of the roller coaster ride that lay ahead. And I was in charge.

I came home that night, excited and scared, still not sure what I had gotten myself into. I was reminded of the days when we were looking to secure the vote for women: all energy but uncertain how to navigate the days ahead. Those 11 years now seemed like a lifetime ago.

Unlike our political agenda, the underlying motivation for this venture was that we all needed the money. The easy earnings during the Great War had quickly evaporated as the lure of labor-saving machinery proved too enticing for the men to purchase. And it was all being bought on credit. Eli was one of the first to get a tractor, and debt on our farm was ever increasing.

We have been able to feed the family, but besides the money I bring home from the market, there was little else. I simply knew we needed more cash to make ends meet. The stories of other farmers who had to walk away from their fields because of debt were being heard much too often. My comrades-in-arms faced the same financial pressures. We had to make this work.

I told Eli about the cooperative after dinner the following night. He was shocked I even entertained a conversation about selling more eggs. He didn't think it would be proper for me to be negotiating prices and entering into any business agreement.

I asked if he had any idea what I did when I went to the market on Wednesdays. How was this any different? He shrugged his shoulders and told me I could do what I liked with the hospital, but that we needed the market money to run the farm. That was the end of the discussion, as he went off to one of his political meetings.

I seethed inside. Why couldn't he be encouraging, even now? Eli continues to see the world—and my place in it—through a lens that has not yet focused on the fact that we are in a different time and I am a different woman than the one he courted in my Mother's parlor. He has never encouraged me to do anything else with my life, other than be a wife and a mother. And Louise is right about me. I have always needed something more. As much as I love my children and understand the role of being a farmer's wife, I have always been searching for something else. In addition to, not because of.

The night before my meeting at the hospital, I stayed with Belle and Stella. They were as energized as I was about the possibilities that potentially lay ahead. By now, I have become quite accustomed to seeing them as a couple, a secret life they keep safely hidden from most of the world.

That morning I couldn't tell if I was excited or nervous; the sensation in my stomach felt the same. My hands shook as I rearranged my hat for the umpteenth time. Belle finally took charge, arranging my hair and skirt so that I was both presentable and professional.

I was about to enter a man's world on behalf of *The Ladies from the Hill*. I had never done anything quite so daring before, and I needed to look the part of a self-assured and competent business woman.

Sheila met me at the hospital and was clearly excited about the possibility of bringing farm fresh products into the kitchen. She confided to me that she hoped a new position would be created, a dietician who would be responsible for integrating nutrition into the patient treatment plan. She explained a number of hospitals were going in that direction and her goal was to lead that same function at Sisters.

As I got caught up in her excitement, my anxiety vanished. The Pharmacy Director was portly and middle-aged, appearing to be stuffed into a chair that barely fit him. His office smelt of chloroform and iodine. He wore old-fashioned clothes, though sharply pressed and crisp. His presence was powerful, and though completely different in look, he strangely reminded me of Mother. I believe it was his eyes; though sharp and intelligent, they were not unkind.

I fell into an easy conversation with him, and in a very short period of time, we agreed on a three-month trial period to be sure the arrangement worked well for all involved. As a retainer fee, I got a check for more money than I had ever seen at one time that allowed us to buy the additional hens and the truck we would need for our enterprise.

Three weeks from that first day, we took this first step on our venture with an optimism that was energizing and a sense of union that women feel when committed to a cause.

Looking back on it now, I remain in awe of all we did. You have to admire farm women: we simply figure out what needs to be done and then go about making it happen. Mary and Rita went on a recruiting expedition and soon we added three new members. We were now a group of eight, all from the church, though not all choir members. Sarah, looking much more in charge of her life than when last I saw her, was among the number joining forces with us.

Not all of us rose to the challenge when asked to join. One of the choir members, prickly by nature, told us she was not going to participate because her husband was convinced we would fail. Trying to keep my temper intact, I cleared my throat while modulating my tone. I looked her squarely in the eye and crafted my response as if she and Eli were one and the same person.

Maybe we've been told that women can't do things so many times that we actually believe it. But not this time.

It was a vow I made to myself. I pulled my shoulders back, kept my eyes straight ahead and walked away.

The Ladies from the Hill began working night and day to make sure our production level met the demand we'd created. Sarah offered a rather decaying, but still functional, shed that we turned into our communal chicken coop. It was an immediate hit. Facing south, it would let us take advantage of the winter sun, but was far enough from the main barn and silos to provide us the space we needed.

We cleaned, hammered and set up the coop within one week's time. The nest boxes had hinged lids we could raise from the outside to collect the eggs; the roosts were installed with tubs that could be pulled through a hinged flap for easy cleaning. We were exhausted and exhilarated. We didn't look much like ladies that final day, but we all agreed that we had never seen anything finer than our collective chicken coop.

Eva brought out a jug of her famous apple cider and we toasted our success. Then we went home to complete the daily chores we had left behind.

Throughout all these days of frenzy, it was James and Belle who gave me the support and tools to forge ahead, to make decisions that had no clear-cut answers, and to appear confident, even when I was unsure of what the next step should be.

To this day, James' letters continue to be encouraging, offering me sound financial advice. In the earliest days, he contacted

Joseph Harrison himself and confirmed he was a man of quality that could be trusted.

Belle was over the moon with the thought that she had started something quite splendid.

It was only at home, at night, that my support system eroded. Eli never asked—and, to be fair, never questioned—what or how I was doing. We were beginning to lead separate lives: he had the farm and his growing involvement in local politics, and I divided my time between our mostly grown children and *The Ladies from the Hill*.

The day we brought the hens together dawned with much tribulation and anxiety, both on our part and the flock's. Hens can be quite territorial, and each chicken, like a child, knows its place from peep-hood and fights to retain its status. Bringing our flocks together was going to be a challenge, and the addition of new chickens would add to the stress.

The eight of us took turns, waiting and watching the hens struggle for position. Within a week's time, the social system was in place, and the pecking order established.

It was not without its moments, as we lost three of our best layers and two of the newly purchased flock in the conflict. Our own miniature Great War had taken place in the corner of Sarah's farm, although our casualties ended up in Sunday dinners.

With two days out to market day, we began the final stages of preparation. Catherine was a godsend. She organized the younger children—Sarah's brood along with the occasional appearance of Louisa's growing herd—to help wash and crate the eggs. She had them singing songs, so they thought it was a game rather than work. Sheer genius from one so young.

Belle got one of her artist protégés to paint a *The Ladies from the Hill* sign to adorn our recent acquisition of a more-than-slightly-used truck. It was colorful and bright and made us look like a true business venture. To this day, that same sign adorns our newer method of transportation.

The day finally came when we were to deliver our eggs for the hospital and begin to sell our market goods as one. I drove the truck with Elizabeth in the front; Mary, Rita, and Eva sat in the back guarding the eggs. What a sight we must have been: all dressed up in our Sunday best, hats attached but a bit skewed from my bumpy handling of the outdated truck.

We created quite the stir when we arrived at the market. Our regular clients were surprised to see we had joined forces as a group. Thanks to Rita's gentle style and pleasing manner, all were soon convinced our prices and our quality would continue to be the same value.

The men who looked to the local businesses to sell their goods were the challenge. They were both rude and crude. Unable to fathom us working as a unit, they were taken aback that we had procured the first contract with a local hospital. Not unlike so many of their counterparts, they didn't understand that this is a new day and women can do more than breed and bake bread.

They snarled and pointed fingers, making lewd and unflattering remarks. At the moment, they didn't appear dangerous, so we ignored them and set out to accomplish what we had come to do.

Eva and Mary went to trade the eggs for the groceries and goods we needed to restock our pantries. Elizabeth's sharp mind and keen wit made our goods a new form of currency, with change paid in cash. I met the messenger from Sisters' Hospital and with no less fanfare handed over our first shipment.

We arrived back at my house giddy with the success of our first outing, yet there was little time to congratulate ourselves on a job well done. We had agreed to take the initial money earned from the hospital and turn it back into the business—more hens meant more eggs that required a bigger coop and egg-sorting devices. Any monies from our regular clients went back to us directly while cash from new customers were proportioned out by the supplier.

This all required more bookkeeping than I imagined, but it remains fun to see all the numbers showing themselves on the ledger pages. We giggled when I put the funds from our joint efforts into the rose painted teapot Belle had given me, seemingly a lifetime ago. *Well, we've got something brewing,* I said with a smile. *It might as well steep in the finest of china.*

Beginning around our fourth week, hateful notes scrawled in charcoal appeared on the windshield of the truck. The first time, we dismissed it as a childish prank. We were fairly certain the culprits were those men from the market who bartered and negotiated with local bakeries and restaurant owners for higher stakes than women typically sought to do.

The second time, the messages were more threatening, and the third time, we came back to find the truck smeared with manure and a note telling us to go back to the kitchen where we belonged. It was clear by their smug looks and sideways glances that the market men were behind this mischief now taking an ugly turn.

To this day, I am not sure whether their actions stemmed from jealousy that we had procured a business relationship with a hospital on such a large scale or whether the mere thought of women banding together for any reason triggered their behavior. It really didn't matter, then or now.

When I spoke to Eli about it, he dismissed my concern as boys just being boys. He reminded me I was now playing for bigger stakes in a rougher world, and I would either have to learn to live with it or get out.

It was Belle and Stella who became outraged when I told them of these incidents at dinner the following Sunday. They equated it to the ridicule and torment the early suffragettes incurred in their fight for women to get the vote.

The following Wednesday, the most amazing thing happened. It makes me laugh out loud even now as I think of it. The day was bright and sunny when Belle's newly purchased roadster drove into the market, top down and all sleek and shiny. Swinging out of the driver's seat was Stella dressed in pants, of all things. She had a rifle nestled on her shoulder and looked like a character from the Western films that Walter so adores. She barely looked at me as she marched over to the area where the men were grouped, mouths agape as they stared at a sight they had never before seen.

I understand some of you don't think us ladies have any right competing with your businesses.

Most of the gang remained tongue-tied, but one of the more

arrogant of the bunch replied: *That's right, little lady. If I can call you that.* His cohorts roared with laughter.

You sure can, my little man, Stella retorted, invoking even more laughter from the men.

So, here's my challenge. Where I come from we meet our rivals head-on and the winner takes all. So, let's have a sharp-shooting contest: if you win, The Ladies from the Hill pack up their eggs and return to their kitchens—no more contracts with hospitals and the like. If you lose, you leave them alone and let them continue. Unharmed and undisturbed.

I was stunned. Stella was putting everything we were working for—including our dreams—on the line. But before I could say a word, one of the young, burly types shouted: *You are on.*

Off he and Stella went to the open-air field, where a shooting gallery was hastily set up. Word quickly spread that a 'duel' was taking place between the men and the ladies. A crowd formed. Someone flipped a coin to start the proceedings; Stella got the call and chose to take the last shot.

As her competitor rose to begin the match, he gave her a quick wink and smirked, *You might not even want to get your rifle ready once I've finished my round.*

Stella just smiled and stroked her rifle like a newborn baby. She looked at him and said, Your *preferred format, both in time and distance.*

He seemed taken aback, and said, *200 meters and three rounds of five shots each. Winner takes all.*

With that, he walked up to the firing line and sent three of his five shots into bull's-eye range.

Our group began a silent prayer as we looked at Stella taking her place on the same line. She cocked the rifle, steadied the handgrip with her non-firing hand, and shot. The bullet hit dead center. We all screamed as the next three shots found their home in the same small circle, the last shot missing its mark by a needle's stitch.

Her opponent, now red in the face, returned to his spot. The heat of the day and the peering eyes of the crowd seemed to rattle him. Out of his next five shots, only two made the bull's-eye. Stella followed with four more perfect shots.

Now, clearly shaken, her opponent raised his rifle and made the first three shots, the last two finding their home somewhere in the adjoining field. Stella returned to her spot. She only needed one more shot to win the match and she got it on her first try.

She turned to her adversary, who by now was clearly stricken with the fact he had been beaten by a woman and beaten clean.

Do you need to see any more from this little lady or have you had enough?

He mumbled he was done. Stella slowly removed the few remaining bullets, and cradling the rifle in her arms, walked over to the group of men, who were looking at the dust on their boots.

Let me be clear, she said. *If I hear of more incidents of harassment to The Ladies from the Hill, I will be back.*

Her eyes moved slowly down their chests to their pants.

And my target won't be a bull's-eye. I anticipate that you will honor your agreement.

She turned her back and walked over to us.

Such an uproar from all the women, and a few of the men, you have never heard. We were shouting and dancing, hugging and crying, all at the same time. Not only can we vote, we can run a business and outshoot any rascal who gets in our way. It was magical.

I pulled Stella over amidst all the fanfare and whispered: *How did you do it?*

Well, Margaret, I grew up in Tucson, Arizona, where toting a gun is a way of life and survival. I have four older sisters; and when I finally appeared five years after the last one had been born, my father had given up any hope of having a son. So, he moved me into that category. I could ride a horse and shoot a rifle before I could recite the alphabet or master my sums. It probably explains why I am the way I am today.

I hugged her deeply, as I whispered for her ears only: *And I wouldn't have you any other way.*

She grinned widely as she whispered back: *And I spent all day Monday and Tuesday at the shooting range practicing. "Never take anything for granted" is the motto of the wild, wild West.*

The men never bothered us again.

The next weeks were not easy, but we soon adapted to the rhythms of our new life. Hours turned into days, days into weeks, and soon the china teapot began to fill up. By the end of our first year, we had paid off our retainer. We began to strategize what competition might be looming to take away our advantage of being the first in line to secure the hospital trade.

Mary started to spend more time at Sisters, trying to understand how the kitchen worked, so we could be of better service. Rita and I met bi-weekly with the Director of the Pharmacy, whom we referred to as "Mr. Director." Our conversations quickly fell into a comfortable rapport. His ease in working with women and respect for their ability to get the job done must have stemmed from all his years working with the nuns at the hospital. They could be formidable, but they were committed to their calling and their patients.

I continued the relationship with the bank, and Elizabeth took on any correspondence or conversations with Mr. Schrader.

As the second fall approached, we worked feverishly to bring electricity into the chicken coop. Elizabeth read that hens could keep on laying eggs as long as they had light. It didn't need to be natural. Hens laying throughout the winter would be a first. Fresh eggs were a rare commodity in the cold season, and Elizabeth was quick to point out that we could receive premium pricing. It was revolutionary, and we would be among the first to do it in our part of the world.

Thus, our first investment was to light the chicken coop. Our husbands thought we were crazy, but we were determined. We found a hired hand who knew how to lay wire to the generator, and he became the first official employee of the cooperative.

We couldn't pay him much, but he rotated his dinner meals at each of our houses, returning to his quarters each evening with at least a half-pie and fresh bread. While he may not have had many wages to show for his work, by the time the project was complete he looked ten pounds heavier and a great deal more content.

Despite our husbands' skepticism, our hens moved into their own well-lit quarters before the days grew too short. When we went to collect the eggs, we were feeling as cocky as the Bantam roosters who strolled our grounds.

But the hens were agitated. Were the bulbs too bright? Had we miscalculated? Could they tell it was artificial light?

In keeping with the adage that "a little child shall lead us," it was Catherine who asked the question: *Can the hens sleep with the light on all night? It makes me stay awake when Rence keeps the bedroom lit.*

We had found the answer to our problem: lights out at 8 p.m. We kept the hens and the school-age children on the same schedule.

That winter, we doubled our egg prices at the market, and the hospital upped their contract as well. We had scored a financial and commercial success.

I wrote to James about our triumph, and he was jubilant. *I want to hear more about your successes and your role as a business woman. We have much in common, Maggie. More than just the ties of family, but a sense of finding our place in the world.*

It was a chilling November afternoon when Eli came by the table as I was finishing the last of the ledgers. The sun was beginning to set and I was rubbing my eyes as the lines on the pages were beginning to blur. The older I get, the more trouble I have reading in the evening light. *Tired, Margaret?* he queried. I jumped, as I had not heard him come in and was surprised by the concern in his voice. *A little,* I responded. I smiled, *I never knew that putting all our chickens in such a basket would take so much work.* Eli chuckled and then his voice grew serious. *You work hard and it shows. I always knew you were smart. Just never quite pictured you making real money. Not that I am complaining; it's good to have cash coming in. This Depression is making everyone poorer.* As I got up, I gave his hand a quick squeeze. I was about to ask him if he wanted to join me in a cup of tea when he abruptly turned around and said he was going into town for a meeting. With a sigh, one that was both tired and sad, I made my way to the stove and put the kettle on. The house was quiet; Catherine was at school, Florence was visiting friends in Buffalo, and the boys were gone. Leon, I believe, for good. Walter, for the moment.

But Eli was right. We were successful in a time that few could say that. The 'teapot' money, as it was becoming known, was growing fast.

Once we felt secure that we had made the proper investments into the business, we turned to making our lives more comfortable.

Our first acquisition made us feel like the true "ladies" our name declared. We bought a luxury beyond our wildest dreams: a Maytag gasoline-powered wringer washing machine. The children were mesmerized the first time they saw it in action for the machine hummed and lurched like a bull ready to mate. But such joy for the eight of us.

Setting aside Monday as laundry day became a ritual of the

past. We organized the use of the machine around the half-day each person needed to spend volunteering for the business. We arrive at the coop's hen house with laundry piled high in our cars or carts. Then, while the clean laundry waves in the breeze to dry, the lady-of-the-hour performs her co-op duties. It is an arrangement that has served us well.

It was the change in Sarah over the years that was my true mark of success. As she grew more confident in what and how she was doing, she returned in full bloom as a contributing member of the cooperative, with opinions and plans of her own.

When the time comes for me to turn over the reins to the next generation, Sarah will quickly and efficiently take charge. She has come into her own, and I smile each time I think of how the little girl who took it upon herself to learn to play the piano is now becoming a leader among her peers.

With all the good news, there were still times I didn't think we would survive, both because of forces among us and around us. But I do believe that God sometimes sends us exactly what we need, when we need it. We only have to embrace the gift. And so it was with Doña Marie Cicerani.

Doña Marie

When the Ciceranis moved into Sheldon, you would have thought the town had been plagued by locusts. Word quickly spread that we were being invaded by Italians with their olive-toned skin, heavy accents and tomatoes simmering on the stove.

Doña Marie first came to choir practice as we were preparing for the Easter celebration. She has a lovely alto voice that fit perfectly into our four-part harmony. However, that initial encounter sparked a minor rebellion that put me front and center in a conflict.

The following day, a small group of women from the choir came to the house and asked to speak with me privately. They began by saying that they personally had no problems with Doña Marie, then went on for more than 20 minutes describing why she would not fit into the choir.

Not like us, said one.

Such strange people, piped in another, *with her strong accent and odd ways.*

As I failed to respond to their insults and innuendoes, their arguments became more intense and more personal.

Italians are criminals, hoodlums and killers. Have you not heard of Al Capone?

I had heard it all before. It was the same vitriol that people said about the Irish, calling us drunks and ne'er-do-wells. I still recall with terror how god-fearing citizens went after their German neighbors during the War.

Memories came flooding back as I remembered how Maria had been treated in the kitchen at the orphanage. Finally, my temper got the best of me. Rather than throwing a punch this time, I threw my hands up in despair and frustration.

And you call yourselves Catholic! I bellowed so loud they all took a step back. *Were you not at the fire when we burned books only because they were written in German? Do you not remember how German stores in Buffalo were boarded up and their patrons tainted as traitors? Is the Pope not Italian?*

I threw down the gauntlet.

If Doña Marie isn't good enough for your choir, then neither am I. I will let Father know of my decision and why. Please understand that I will give him the names of those women who are Christian in name only. He may need time to determine a sufficient penance for such hypocrisy and uncharitable ways.

With that, I walked over to the door and opened it to show them the way out. They were all over themselves as they got up to leave. I was overreacting, they claimed. I had misinterpreted what they were trying to say. It was not them, but the others they were speaking for.

I said nothing more than that I would be at choir practice and would have Doña Marie with me. If that was unacceptable to the choir, they could continue without both of us. I turned my back and returned to the kitchen.

Eli was as put out as I when I shared the events of the day. I believe he remembers all too well the hurts that were thrust on the Germans just a few short years ago. He nodded as he drank his evening's coffee.

Doña Marie's husband, Salvatore, is a good man and a great barber. We need more hard-working people in this town, whether they are farmers or tradesmen.

I kissed him gently on the top of his thinning hair. *I agree. May we not be the only ones who feel this way.*

The day of choir practice, Catherine and I arrived with Doña Marie at our side. All the ladies were assembled, and not a word was exchanged. We simply had our practice, and all has stayed the same, with the addition of a beautiful alto voice.

It was my friendship with Doña Marie that changed the course for *The Ladies from the Hill*. We were in our fourth year of operation, and our idea was no longer a novelty. As more and more farms developed cooperatives, the initial dealings between the farmer's wives and the merchants began to change. The "city women" were no longer frequenting the markets with any regularity, despite Rita's best efforts.

The one-on-one relationship piece of the business was ebbing away. In this new world, there was only talk of contracts and commitments. Added to this was increased competition from the businesses that were buying out our neighbors' farms from families who either no longer wanted to work the land or could not afford to maintain the small farmer role.

And we were getting tired. The women who had been the heart and soul, as well as the hands that ran the cooperative, were getting older. The rituals of farming life that we grew up with continued to erode. The barn raisings and harvest sharing were more and more a thing of the past.

Other than Louisa, our older children were yearning to follow their friends for the glamour of city jobs and city life. We were becoming more and more isolated, and the strains of that isolation were beginning to pull at the fabric of *The Ladies from the Hill*.

One late spring afternoon, Doña Marie unexpectedly appeared on my doorstep. She had never been involved with the cooperative, as her family were not farmers and kept only the necessary livestock to feed their growing clan.

Margaret, she began in her accent that still sounded like the warm country she had come from. *You are the doyenne of these Ladies from the Hill, correct?*

I started to explain we were a cooperative, that we shared responsibility, but she raised her hand to stop me.

I hear you talk about how it is different today than before. Women in the city now have refrigerators and often don't need to come to the market each week. Near Salvatore's barber shop there is this Loblaw's, a big grocery store that the women come to. No more Wednesday market—now they shop whenever they want for whatever they want. That is not good for your business.

I agreed with everything she said, though I didn't comment.

She continued, *So you have to fill a need these grocery stores can't match. And such an idea I have.*

I nodded and waited to hear more.

Those women who have money want lovely things for their home without having to make these things themselves. We have beautiful gardens with flowers that bloom from spring into the cold weather. And you should check with your sister Belle—how much time do she and her friends spend in the kitchen? If they even know where one is, she chuckled.

My mind was racing. Doña Marie was going in a direction I had never contemplated, but I was eager to see where her journey could take us.

So, Margaret, let us give these women beautiful things that we make and sell to them. Fresh flowers for their tables, your lovely sachets for their bedroom closets. Then perhaps, give them dinner in a basket to take home.

My sachets? The Bavarian Family Secret? Dinner in a basket? I understood what Doña Marie was proposing; it was so much more than anything we had ever done or imagined.

Doña Marie was on a mission, and I let her continue.

Why don't you propose to your ladies that next week we bring bouquets of flowers from our gardens to the market and see if they sell. The same with dinners in a basket. I will be the first to try this. Should they sell, we do more. And then your sachets. I have an idea about special Christmas presents we can do. But that is for another day. First, the flowers.

I called Elizabeth that night, telling her there may be a new direction for *The Ladies from the Hill* that I wanted to discuss with her. She readily agreed to meet the next morning as there was something she needed to tell me as well.

I couldn't sleep that night, excited about the possibilities that Doña Marie was proposing, while concerned about what Elizabeth needed to share.

Once it was outlined, Elizabeth's mind quickly saw the potential of Doña Marie's proposal.

Simply brilliant, she said. *We are struggling to keep the business we have known and grown intact. This gives us a new avenue without a great deal of investment. Let's meet with the others after choir practice and lay out the plan. One step at a time.*

And then she paused.

Well, Elizabeth, I said. *What is it you have kept from me?*

Her cheeks burned pink as she burst out the news: *Ray and I are to get married! He asked me last week, and I said yes.*

This was not at all what I was expecting, and my first question was, *Who is Ray?*

Why, Mr. Schrader, Elizabeth replied, looking at me incredulously.

I couldn't believe my ears. Elizabeth's husband, Walter, had died after a long illness more than two years ago. She had stayed on at the farm with her son and daughter-in-law and had seemed quite content in the arrangement. I asked the obvious questions: *what, how when?*

She giggled as she recounted their courtship; first, a series of phone calls to discuss the business that didn't seem really necessary. She hadn't suspected he was interested in her until he asked her out to dinner. From that date on, it was but three short months until he asked her to marry him.

He is quite lovely, she bubbled. *He was widowed many years ago when his wife died in childbirth. He is looking forward to belonging to a family, though I don't believe my boys will be keen on my being with someone who isn't their father. Not sure they have thought of me and their father performing the marriage act, though now with all four of them married with children of their own they should know that there is no such thing as finding a baby under a cabbage leaf.*

She turned bright red, and I hugged her tightly. *I couldn't be happier for you. You deserve all the joy that you can find in this life.*

She asked if I would stand by her side when she and Ray said their vows. *You are the closest thing I have to a sister, Margaret. Working with you and watching The Ladies from the Hill grow and flourish is like being among family to me.*

And I did. On their wedding day, I looked over at Eli as I stood at the altar. It was if I was seeing him for the first time in all these many years. Eli's shoulders remain straight while the rest of him has begun to sag. His hair is backing away from his forehead. Growing old, with all its disappointments, is wearing him away. Like the soil in the fields, he is getting used up by the demands that have been placed on him. He finds no solace in the world that is changing around him and I don't know how to make it right for him.

Elizabeth and Ray were committing to spend the rest of their years together. A bond of love, shared expectations and a future they would both participate in. When Eli and I made our vows, I thought I could marry someone I liked, and we would have a happy family. That has not been how it turned out.

Eli and I remain together more out of obligation than love, or just because neither of us has another choice. Perhaps it was my life with the Ladies from the Hill that took me further and further away from the farm and him. It was not the miles that distanced us—I was energized by a life that was exciting and modern. Eli's life was dwindling, piece by piece.

I smiled tenderly as I looked at Elizabeth. I am happy for her and somewhat envious. She is loved and in love. I cannot say the same.

At the luncheon following the ceremony, Ray winked as he whispered somewhat conspiratorially that he would now be working for *The Ladies from the Hill* at no cost, for we had given him the greatest reward ever, his Elizabeth. I basked in the glow of their happiness at having found each other while my heart ached for not having such love in my life. I went to search for Eli and found him encircled by his fellow political cronies. There seems to be a connection between his growing involvement in town politics and his drinking. That day was no exception. As I walked over to the group, he barely looked up at me, making no effort to join me at any point. When I found him at the end of the party, he had clearly had too much to drink. I drove us home, feeling more alone than I have felt since Da abandoned Nell and me on the orphanage steps. You can live with someone, bear their children and their heartaches, and still feel forsaken. You can still feel alone in the world even with them by your side.

In the midst of all my jumbled feelings, *The Ladies from the Hill* charted their new course. The initial bouquets Doña Marie assembled were breathtaking: lavenders and pinks tied with burlap string that made them look like a piece of a country garden.

For our first Meal in a Basket, she took jars of her tomato sauce she called "gravy," along with homemade pasta and bread. The Basket was sold before we could even find room for it on the table.

We made our new beginnings a resounding success.

Thanksgiving and Christmas offered new opportunities to raise money in ways we never thought probable. Christmas wreaths, trees made of pine cones and holly. Women were buying crafts our children had been making for years. The teapot overflowed.

The sachets, however, were another story. The secret was not mine to share. I had to get my Mother's permission.

It was an odd day for January, as the sun belied the calendar.

Though we are still in the midst of another unforgiving winter, there was an unexpected warm breeze as I made my way to my Mother's grave.

When she first died, I would find myself sitting here, talking to her as if she was working her needle and thread and I was at the kitchen table trying to copy her every move. After Catherine, I found I couldn't find the words to tell her what had happened or how I had felt. Michael may have given me absolution, but I have not felt contrite for loving a man I cannot have, nor for betraying the man I call my husband.

I approached her grave with my head down, not knowing what I was going to do or say. As I started to brush the dried leaves from the grass encroaching on her stone, a calmness came over me. It was not unlike the feeling I got in my early days with her, when the uncertainties of where I was and how I could belong might overwhelm me. I would find Mother wherever she was. No words were needed. She gave me a sense of peace and comfort by being near her.

A cardinal, his red breast a spark of color against the crisp blue sky, appeared in a far-off tree. And though no words were spoken, I confessed my sins, those of commission and those of omission. Then I began to weep, salty tears that released all the ache and sense of loss that I had bottled up inside me.

When I was done, I felt stronger and braver than I had in years. Mother either forgave me or understood me. I do not know nor care which. I just knew I was going to be okay. I knew she was still my protector and my guide. Why had I ever doubted her?

That was two days ago. I returned to writing in this journal the very next day.

Belle

In the midst of all this sadness and uncertainty, Belle is no longer at my side.

During those years when the world of finance tumbled down, and the country sank deeper into this terrible Depression, I worried about Belle and how this might impact her. Once I got up the nerve to inquire, she told me not to worry.

In her travels, she met an Irish rogue from Boston.

You would love him, Margaret, she said. *He is bright, brash, bold and fun—and married to the Mayor's daughter. Years ago, he told me to get out of the stock market and invest my money in real estate, liquor, and movie studios. I never understood how stocks made money. Land and beer—that rings true to my heritage.*

No need to worry about me. Stella and I won't be any of your poor relations coming with hat-in-hand needing your Sunday dinner. I will continue to come to simply share your fine cooking and cheery company.

The call of the glamour and glitter of Hollywood became more than a financial investment. Two years ago, Belle and Stella packed their bags and boarded a train for California. Stella, who had been writing Western short stories for one of the local magazines, had caught the eye of Frances Marion, a screenwriter who works with Mary Pickford. Frances who fancies herself a journalist despite her Hollywood awards, asked Stella to work with her as a screenwriter.

When they came home for Christmas the first year, Stella glowed as she told of her work.

Margaret, I actually become the characters I am writing about. I see the world through their eyes: loving who they love, fighting their battles with steadfast determination and valor. I simply put my dreams on papers and people pay me an extraordinary sum of money to do what I love. And I never seem to run out of stories to tell.

Belle fell in love with California.

It is so unlike Buffalo . . . flowers unlike any you have imagined bloom with such vibrant tints they make my beloved French paintings dim in comparison. There is seldom a cloud in the sky, and the women use umbrellas, properly named "parasols," to keep their pale skin protected from the unrelenting sun.

Mountains dominate a landscape that leads you to tumultuous waves, and their ocean is anything but Pacific. Amid all this beauty is the movie business, a world that fits Stella for, like her, it is both unchartered and exciting.

Walter, in particular thought it glamorous to have an aunt living in California. He would join the girls and I at the North Park Theatre and sit in amazement as one of Stella's movies was featured. There, on the screen, her words turned into images, bringing the audience to a place they never dreamed possible, physically and emotionally. It is a new world, and I am not sure how well I fit into it.

It was not only the glamour of Hollywood that made my

children swoon. In true Belle form, the summer after her first year out West, Belle rented a house in the Finger Lakes for the month of July. There was a standing invitation for all her nieces and nephews to join her for a "cousins' memory." She told me she missed the young people in her life and wanted to be sure they would always remember her.

They all went; some together, like Louise and Frank, and some, like Leon, alone. My flock returned with sunburned faces and sun-bleached hair, and tales of leisure days and fun-filled evenings. None, not even Catherine, gave the slightest details of what had transpired.

Yet the experience seemed to forge a special bond among them, despite the age differences. Belle had once again charmed all.

When she returned, I tugged her arm and wanted more details.

So, my dear Belle, tell me what was it like with all those young people for so many days and nights.

With twinkling eyes, she sighed: *It was magical.*

And that was that.

James

My heart breaks for the brother I have not seen in years, but who has been a constant source of support and love for me. I have kept most of his letters. My most recent, dated this October, tells of an unrelenting sadness that permeates his days and keeps him from rest at night.

My Dear Sister,

This letter brings only the saddest of news. My own dear boy, my Jimmy, died in an airplane crash at an airstrip near Portmarnock one week ago. His plane hit a tree, crashed and caught fire. We buried him—or what was left of him —yesterday.

The day of the funeral was bitterly cold. A thick, pervasive atmosphere of grief settled into the pews of the church like a fog. You could touch the sorrow, as it hushed the church so the only sound was the echoing of the cruel wind beating against the stained-glass windows.

Annie is like a ghost, a woman merely going through the motions expected of her, but whose vacant eyes reflect the emptiness of her soul, mourning a love that has been snatched so abruptly and cruelly.

Our grief is overwhelming. I am angry at God for letting men take to flying in the skies. I am angry at God for taking the light from our life. I am angry at God for taking away my future.

I do not know if Annie and I can survive this heartbreak. The pain is unbearable.

Your grieving brother,

James

November

There is also heartbreak when a son is not a part of your life.

Eli has always seen his future clearly. He knew what was

expected. He plants a seed, and either it flourishes or it withers. In his world, there is no misfortune he can foresee that cannot be countered with toil and sweat. Without ever saying it, he simply knows he will die on this land and be buried in the cemetery next to the church.

He has always assumed that his son, and his son's sons would work the fields that generations of George men had farmed. Leon's rejection of all this is unthinkable to him. It is as if, in rejecting the land, Leon has somehow rejected Eli and all he has stood for.

Leon returned home, but only because he needs a roof over his head and food at the table. He does only what is required and appears to have little sense of what he wants, only what he wants no part of.

I do not know how to resolve the strife between him and his father.

In my heart, I know this has nothing to do with me. I watch Leon rant and rave, much like I saw him as a toddler, thrashing about and screaming until exhausted. Now he is a man. And the fights between Eli and him are getting louder and crueler.

He calls his father "stupid," and Eli spits out the words "ungrateful" and "lazy." This is not the way that our life was to evolve. Somehow, I think Eli blames me that Leon wants a different life. The smell of the soil in the spring and the harvesting of crops in the fall define Eli. He is, and always has been, one with the land. To have a son, his first-born and rightful heir to this same land, reject it is a burden and heartache. Eli doesn't talk about that. It is simply easier to yell.

Over the years, I have tried to get Eli to see that while he has no qualms badgering Leon when he does something wrong, he seldom congratulates him on the things he does well. When I talk to Leon, I attempt to make him realize that his father is a good man. And like all of us, he is mortal and flawed. My arguments, in both cases, fall on deaf ears. They are too much alike, believing there is no compromise. Their way is the only way.

Two weeks ago, the battle escalated. I am not sure what started the fight and no one has offered up the details.

I was finishing the lunch dishes when I heard Catherine screaming my name from the barn. I came rushing in to find Eli looking as if he wanted to spear Leon with the pitchfork he held above his head. Leon was on the floor, bloodied and bruised, with no fight left in him.

I shrieked and flew into the only spot where I could prevent the unthinkable from happening. As I stood between the two of them, I looked straight into Eli's eyes. They were black with rage. I had never seen him like this before. The strength that had seemed to be waning all these past months was now resurrected as if stirred by some outside evil force.

I spoke calmly: *For the love of Jesus, Eli, drop the pitchfork. Enough harm has been done for the day.*

Eli stared back at me and finally threw the pitchfork aside. He turned and walked down the road.

Catherine and I brought Leon to the house where I bandaged

his wounds. Leon never said a word about what happened. When he had regained enough strength to stand on his own, he went back to his room. Minutes later, he came into the kitchen with his satchel over his shoulders. *I am leaving.*

He left without saying goodbye to his brother and sisters. No one said a word at the dinner table and the meal was eaten in silence.

Eli came home hours later, smelling of liquor. I said nothing as he slammed his way around the house, muttering such terrible things as if the devil himself had taken possession of his soul. I moved from his bed into Leon's room that night and have not returned.

I am not sure how much and how often Eli is drinking. And not just a glass or two of beer, but rather hard liquor. He doesn't do it in the house, so I have something to be thankful for.

December

My Beloved Sister,

The worst has come: Annie died earlier this week. She had grown increasingly weak, unable to swallow the smallest sip of water. I think she gave up on life after Jimmy died.

I am now totally alone in the world, if it were not for you.

I am not sure I can continue with this burden of life.

I am in despair.

James

We are thousands of miles away and I long to hold him in my arms and provide some comfort. Our lives are so very different; our fortunes not the same. For the moment, all I can do is pray.

And while I cannot fathom his loss, I know the emptiness of a family no longer intact. Florence has moved to East Aurora to finish her education. Eli raised no objection. Yesterday, Walter announced he is taking the train to California. He believes the movies could be his to conquer. So off he is going to find his way to Belle's, though Stella is the one he wants to see. Eli said nothing, merely grunted and walked out the door.

Only Catherine is left at home. The walls are strangely silent. There is no laughter, no shouts of greeting. Eli has left me in spirit. Only Catherine's presence provides the buoy to keep me from drowning.

January

Teaching *The Ladies from the Hill* how to make the sachets was not as heart-wrenching as I had anticipated. In fact, it all went surprisingly well. I began by telling the story of my Grande Tante, and there was a great deal of chuckling and knowing glances when I spoke of the elopement.

Too many of us had daughters who strayed from the path to be shocked at a young woman swept away by a passionate kiss from a handsome young buck.

When I assembled the oils on the table around which we had gathered, there was a collective sigh of acknowledgement as I revealed this one ingredient that made the difference. Mary's laughter filled the room:

At last, the secret is out. I knew it had to be something special and after all these years, the answer to the question was this simple. Capturing the oil from the flower is what keeps the scent alive. So basic, and yet, who knew?

April

It is early spring, the lilacs are in full bloom, and we have harvested and dried the leaves. *The Ladies from the Hill* met to assemble the first of our sachets. We want to have them ready to sell as Mother's Day gifts. There was a great deal of enthusiasm when we told our customers they were going to be able to have the fresh smells of the garden with them all year along.

After adding the precious oil to bounty of leaves and petals we had so carefully dried, we looked at the pieces of fabric we each brought. The table became clothed in myriad colors and textures. We picked out the fabrics that would work the best —open enough to capture the fragrance, but with a tight weave so the dried leaves and petals couldn't fall through.

We began to stitch and talk, a welcome respite from our relentlessly busy world. As I looked around the table, I understood once again the gift of true and binding sisterhood. There was no pretense among us, no concern about how we acted or how we looked. When I am with these women, I can feel myself breathe.

June

The sachets were a great hit at the market. We simply cannot keep up with the growing demand. It was Sarah, having taken over Elizabeth's role as the business person in the group, who posed the idea of buying a sewing machine.

We don't need to purchase a new one. Think how lovely it would be not to be enslaved by the needle. We can more than meet the demand, and can get our older daughters to help out.

I checked the 'teapot' money; we had close to $100.00. From what Sarah had learned, that would buy us a good second-hand Singer.

I will see what I can find, if we agree we should purchase one.

Sarah got nods of approval from all around the table and a new venture had begun.

She came back the following week having met the objective. The sewing machine was jet-black, decorated with apple blossom and cornflower decals with wrought-iron legs connected in an intricate, web-like pattern. Walnut inserts in the front of the oak cover lent it the air of a valuable piece of furniture.

Collectively we thought it was the grandest thing we had ever seen. To no longer have the yoke of needle and thread tying us down was a glorious feeling. We simply had to make the payment and the Singer would belong to us.

I went home and walked straight to the teapot to get the money. The bills that last week had been so tightly bound by a rubber band were carelessly thrown into the pot. $30.00 was missing. We didn't have enough money to pay for the machine.

I kept recounting the bills, as if the mistake was mine rather than the unthinkable. But someone had taken it. All I could think of was that Eli had to know.

I found him in the barn tending a cow that had fallen ill. When I asked if he knew what had happened, he shrugged his shoulders and said he had needed the money. I choked out the word, *Why?*

He shouted, *I told you I needed it! Damn foolishness, you and your teapot money. You are my wife, and I can take whatever I want from you whenever I want it. You would have nothing if it weren't for me—including a roof over your head and food for your table. I needed the money. I took it and I am finished with this conversation.*

He turned his back and went back to the sick cow.

Rage, confusion and sadness ran through me, but this was not the time to let my emotions take hold. I needed to think, not feel. Shaking, I went back to the house.

My first thought was to call Belle, but my pride wouldn't let me. Eli was her brother and, no matter how awful his transgression, I did not want her to know what he had done.

I began working in the garden, pulling at weeds and tilling the soil with a fierceness fueled by my sense of betrayal. As I surveyed the rolling hills and lush green beauty surrounding me, a quiet calmness came over me.

I ran a business and I would treat this as a business transaction. I placed a phone call to Mr. Harrison at the bank. I would get a loan for the needed money and pay it back from my share of the profits over time.

And that is what I did. Mr. Harrison assured me of my

credibility, and given my excellent credit rating, he gave me the best terms he could offer for a loan without any collateral to back it up. I went home with the cash in hand and went immediately to Sarah's farm.

Sarah took the carefully counted bills and within the week, the sewing machine was purchased. The sachet business was now in full throttle, but my sense of loss was overwhelming. The Bavarian family secret was now common knowledge, and as lovely as the sachets were, they had lost their magic for me.

Eli had stolen more from me than money. Despite all I had done, how hard I had worked and the successes we had accomplished, he did not respect me. I felt an emptiness I can't describe.

I know the world is not as he would like, nor as he planned. It was a simpler world 30 years ago—with neighbors at our door, helping us in every way. Our expectations and our dreams were limited. We wanted nothing else for our children but what we had achieved ourselves. There was no talk of having more or of wanting more.

Only Louise fits his picture of how children should behave. Leon and Walter have left the farm. Florence will continue to forge a new path. Catherine will use her as a model for whatever she does next. There are brighter lights and more opportunities outside these acres that belong to their heritage.

Eli never wanted these changes, and they have all happened too quickly for him. He was never unkind or cruel, but these days are wearing him down. There is a bitterness brewing in him like milk that has been left too long and slowly begins to curdle. He is slowly souring on life, on me, and all that we have done together.

Taking the money was not an act of vengeance. I believe he thinks what is mine is rightfully his because I am his wife. In his view, my status in the world is only because of him, not because of anything I have accomplished.

This breaks my heart more than anything else.

September

I am rocked to the core. The conversation started simply enough with Mary asking me if I had heard the news about Father Michael. The blood must have drained from my face as I was shaking my head 'no'; Mary paused to ask if I was alright. I tried to smile and made some remark about the plight of middle-aged women. *Father Michael?* I mumbled.

Ah, yes, was her response. *One of the men had heard at the Knights of Columbus meeting in Buffalo that, in July, Father Michael had been seriously wounded in a riot in Belfast. According to the story, the Protestants hold this big celebration there called the Orange Parade that touts their victory at the Battle of Borne. The Catholics living there are being driven out of their jobs and homes, and so they started to jeer at the marchers and a huge fight broke out.*

Father Michael was in the midst of it all, trying to get both sides to settle down. He was beaten by a gang of thugs and left on the church steps. They said he was barely alive when they brought him into the rectory.

I couldn't breathe. *Is he alive?*

No one knows for sure, Mary replied. *But we think we should organize a bake sale to raise money for those poor folks who have lost their homes only because they were baptized in the one true Church. It is sad times we are living in, Margaret.*

I don't remember what I answered or how I got home. The world became blurry.

I wrote to James that night to see if he could find any news. His letter came yesterday.

> *My Dear Maggie,*
>
> *I write quickly as I know you are worried about your former pastor. I am afraid my news is not the happiest.*
>
> *The riots in Belfast seldom make headlines here in Dublin; though connected by language and land, we are worlds apart. So, I could not find any news about your Father Michael through my normal channels—the newspapers or the men at my club.*
>
> *I thought my best source would be our parish priest who holds the rank of Monsignor and would have a better handle on the trials the Catholics are facing in Ulster. I gave him the particulars as you described and he came by the house last night with the news.*
>
> *The best we have is that Father Michael was singled out that particular night and beaten as an example to others who are standing up for the injustices that continue to be cast upon our Catholic brethren. Although Father Michael was not about the politics engulfing both sides, he has the reputation of hating violence at anyone's hand. But that was not enough for these*

brutes. Your priest was badly beaten, then left on the church steps, bleeding and broken.

A local churchwoman found him and if it were not for her, according to Monsignor, he would have died then and there.

He was brought into the rectory and a local doctor was called. That is the last piece of the story the public has been told.

Monsignor believes—and he is a man who knows his way around the doings of the Church—that Father Michael was taken to the monastery in Clonard run by the Redemptorists, a congregation of priests and brothers who live in community. There, he will be able to heal and eventually lead a life of quiet reflection and prayer. Monsignor was clear that his role as an intermediary between these warring factions is over for he will never be a well man again.

We are thankful that his name is not but one more to be put on the list of martyrs for the cause of freedom in Ireland.

Father Michael sounds like an incredible man, both priest and peacemaker. I would have liked to have made his acquaintance.

Keep him and this land of ours in your prayers, Maggie. I fear Father Michael will not be the last to suffer for the love of his countrymen.

With love and affection,

Your brother,

James

I sighed with both relief and pain. Michael was alive, but

horribly wounded. When I think back to that day with him, so many years ago, it seems unreal. Yet I can remember each line of his face so clearly and the gentleness of his touch.

To think he has suffered such cruelty makes me question how God could ever let this happen. My faith is being stretched thin. I can find no answer to bring me comfort.

October

Eli is drinking more and more. He comes in from his chores, eats his meal, and then it is either back to the barn or off to attend a political meeting in the village. By the time he gets home, it is dark, and he is drunk.

Those few times I am still awake, I hear him slur his words and see his unsteady gait. I am afraid to speak up, though, as we simply do not talk about such things anymore. Our conversations are about the daily needs of the house, my continued bookkeeping on the farm outputs, and updates on the children. Our relationship is no longer a partnership of life, but more of property managers. And the children are part of Eli's property.

March

Just when I thought that my heart could not bear any more with Eli's continued drinking, I looked up from the kitchen table to see Belle standing in my doorway. She looked haggard and worn out, her blue silk traveling dress hanging on her as if it were borrowed from a woman twice her size.

As I hugged her, hoping to revive my strength by her sheer

presence, I felt her bones, sharp and brittle through the tender fabric.

Why didn't you tell me you were coming? I mumbled in her ear.

I could barely hear her response: *I have come home, Margaret. I have come home to die.*

I stopped breathing. This must be a bad dream. I don't have the strength to take much more.

I said nothing as Belle went on.

I have cancer. A very aggressive form that is eating me up from the inside. The doctors in California told me I have less than three months to live. That was a month ago. I want to die at home. California's bright blue skies and never-ending sunshine is not the backdrop I want for my last days on earth.

And she smiled the Belle smile that I love so well.

My vision blurred as I looked across the table at the woman who has been my protector, my guide, my sister. This couldn't be true. A world without Belle would have no color, no joy, no spontaneity. Tears slid down my cheeks, and I couldn't catch my breath. I finally whispered, *Stella.*

Belle just shook her head.

She needs to be in California. There is no place for her at my bedside as I enter my own personal purgatory. We said our final goodbye as I got on the train to come to you. I wanted to leave her when I could hold her in my arms one last time. She eventually understood that the decision was mine to make. It was her last gift to me. Walter is staying with us, so she is not alone.

Sobbing, I reached for her hand. Once so graceful and

manicured, her fingers were now curling into her palms, the nails yellow and brittle.

What are we to do? I choked out.

It is all arranged, she replied. *I have a nurse with me and we will hire more once I am settled. Leon has opened the house and is living there now. He will stay with me. You can come later this week to see that all is settled and then I will have no more visitors. Even you, Margaret. I have enough of my own pain to bear without seeing the pain in your eyes.*

I didn't know what I was more shocked to hear: that Belle had come home to die, or that Leon and she had been in touch. *What, how?*

I have known for years about Leon's desire to leave the farm. He has to find time away from all of this to figure out who he is and what he wants. Even before this last falling out with Eli, he had asked if he could stay at my house. I agreed. Now, it all seems like a perfect solution to an imperfect situation. I told him I would tell you, and you could let Eli know the best way possible.

I have a car and driver outside and am on my way home now. I will call and let you know when you can come to visit. I have much to do to get my affairs in order.

She looked away as she added: *I always thought I would have more time.*

And then she shrugged: *But that is not God's plan. We are where we are, and it is what it is. I have some time left, and you need to buy a new black dress.*

And with that, she kissed my cheek, waved her hand, and leaning on a cane I hadn't seen when she entered, she left. I knew it would be the last time I would see that silhouette frame my doorway.

I fell on my knees, not knowing what to do next. I saw Eli walking to the barn and followed him in. When I told him about Belle, his eyes filled with tears, but there were no words of comfort coming my way.

Well, we are getting to be at that age, Margaret. Our friends are going to die. We might as well get used to it. I am glad she is home. It is where she has always belonged.

And with that, he went about his chores.

I will not tell him about Leon. It will not help matters between them, and I don't have the strength to bear his anger.

April 22nd

Belle is gone.

It is only 10 days since I saw her for the last time. She was frail, but her spark was still there. She had ordered three ready-made black dresses for me to try on. I told her I would do no such thing; I had no intention of preparing to mourn her while she was still here giving me orders.

She smiled. *Margaret, it is not like you to hide your head in a bushel basket. I want to be sure you look proper to present yourself as my true sister. Death will never break the bond we share. Try each on and I will decide what suits you best.*

And that is what we did. It felt like I was in a hazy dream: Belle telling me how to pull the brim of the hat just so to transform an ordinary cloche into the latest in fashion, the "slouch" hat. We settled on a dress with a zipper—no more buttons and snaps for the likes of me—and with wide shoulder pads that did their very best to make my expanding hips and waist look smaller.

As I looked at myself in the mirror, I wondered who this woman with salt-and-pepper hair and eyes red-rimmed from crying actually was. But Belle allowed me no time to wallow in my self-pity. When she was finally satisfied with how I would look, she laid back on the pillow.

Come say goodbye. I am tired. Take these things, and then start your house cleaning. When the time comes, I will be laid out at your house. It was my first home, you know. And I shall be buried in Sheldon near my mother and father. John's mother made sure there was no room in the family plot for the likes of me.

With a twinkle still in her eyes, she continued, *I doubt she and I will meet up again. I intend to be in heaven.*

Then she held my gaze, *Leave me in peace, my dearest sister. All is arranged. Leon has the details.*

And she closed her eyes.

I knelt at her bed and brought her hand to my lips.

How will I live without you?

Then I prayed as I haven't prayed since Michael left, asking God for strength to carry on. I am not sure even now that I can manage.

When Leon called to say that Belle had passed, he told the most amazing story. He had gone to her bed to give the nurse a break. Belle had not been eating or drinking and was in and out of consciousness.

As he was sitting at her bedside, she sat straight up. She opened her eyes, extended her arms and shouted: *Ready!*

With that, she took her last breath and was gone. I can only imagine that the Lord had come to her personally to welcome her to his heavenly home. And that thought has helped to mend my heart that feels like it is broken in too many pieces.

April 25th

Belle has been laid to rest. She had everything planned for this, her final soiree. The funeral director delivered the casket, flowers, and a list of the hymns and gospel passages to be read at the Mass.

I relinquished my role as soloist for Belle's funeral to Catherine. She sang the *Ave Maria* and was in superb voice: pure, rich and mellow at the same time. It reminds me of the fine wines Belle would pour at her fancy dinners—an unexpected burst of pleasure when it is first sipped with the memory remaining after the glass has been drained.

Despite my breaking heart, I held my breath as Catherine paused slightly before making her plea to the Virgin. Her *Ave Maria* was more tender, more heartfelt than mine. The church echoed with the notes both vibrant and prayerful.

I raised my hands to the others and our voices rose for the final chorus, all separate and all as one. Then a peacefulness that was both poignant and exhilarating descended upon us. I smiled at Catherine and nodded.

Leon came home for Belle's funeral, and Walter took a train from California, traveling day and night to arrive on time. The entire family was together for the first time in years. As we walked silently and respectfully, following the casket from the altar to the grave site, I was content, an emotion I have not felt for a very long time. Belle was gone, but her spirit would remain with me forever. She was in a better place; my faith affirmed that. And I believed heaven was a bit more vibrant now that Belle had taken up residency.

Belle had paid Doña Marie to bring the food to the church hall once the casket had been lowered into the freshly dug grave. It was like no other funeral that Sheldon had ever seen —a party for rejoicing rather than grieving. Belle was Belle to the end. There will never be another quite like her.

July

The most amazing thing has happened. Ray asked me to come by his law office as soon as I was free. Three days later, we met. After we exchanged the initial pleasantries about his life with Elizabeth and the change in direction for *The Ladies from the Hill*, he got to the business at hand.

Belle had died a wealthy woman, having taken the monies she inherited following John's death and investing them wisely. Ray explained that I was her only living beneficiary. Specifically, she has left me $5,000—an extraordinary sum.

Ray went on to explain that the remainder of her monies were split between a foundation advancing the role of women in this country and a trust fund she had arranged for the education of her nieces and nephews.

Taken aback by the news of my newly found wealth, I had the presence of mind to ask more about the trust fund. As always, Ray was straightforward, foregoing all the legal talk to describe simply what Belle had intended and how it was to work.

A fair amount of money was established that any of her nieces and nephews (and future generations) could use for their education. If one of them wished to receive the education funds, they would meet with either him or Mr. Harrison, who were the appointed trustees, to ensure that the conditions of the trust were being met. Then all would be taken care of.

This was so Belle: giving people an opportunity, but not a handout. My thoughts went immediately to my children and grandchildren. This last gesture on Belle's part could make a difference in their lives. And her gift to me was going to make a difference in mine.

I already knew how it was to be spent: I was going to pay off my loan and redo the inside of the house. I was still living in rooms that looked essentially the same as the day I moved in. It is time that I make them look like mine.

Eli went into a rage when I told him what Belle had done. He does not value school beyond what the village provided. After ranting that his children were not going to be "educated fools," he demanded that I hand over the money Belle had left me.

I simply told him no. This is my money, and I was going to spend it on the house and not the barn. He had stolen the money from the teapot that I was still paying back, but he was not going to get his hands on what is rightfully mine.

He shouted I was his wife and whatever was mine was his to do with as he pleased.

I couldn't control my temper and shouted back: *Not anymore and never again.*

He shook his fist, and for a moment, I thought he was going to strike me. Then Catherine walked in; Eli's eyes shifted to her, and his hand dropped to his side.

We are not done with this conversation, Margaret.

He left. I don't know where he went, and I don't care.

February

I have stepped aside from my leadership role with *The Ladies from the Hill.* It is time. They have expanded their reach and their resources, and while it has been exciting to see it grow and develop, new leadership and energy are needed. I am tired and, like so many things in life, it is time to move on.

Eva and Mary are no longer a part of the group, as they moved away. Their husbands have given up farming and all that goes with that life.

Sarah has naturally assumed the leadership role, and new women, including Doña Marie, have been integrated into the group. I will stay on for a while, along with Rita. We will be the glue, bridging the old and the new worlds. It is not the same. And it should not be.

When I see the teapot, I am reminded of what women can accomplish. When we believe in something, we come together to make it happen. In this same way, I believe that

Florence and Catherine will continue to grow and learn together. I pray Louise's daughters also catch the spark of that same flame so they can become all that they are capable of.

April

This morning I woke to find Eli passed out on the kitchen floor. When I tried to rouse him, he became belligerent, like a caged animal that suddenly had been poked. I finally got him into his bed before Catherine came down.

I cannot have her seeing him this way. I cannot bear seeing him this way.

July

My Dear Maggie,

For all these many years we have been writing, like the brother and sister that we are, sharing each other's joys and sorrows.

I now know I am not a well man. It was at my annual physical that I learned the diagnosis. Though I have lacked the energy and stamina that I once enjoyed, I blamed it on melancholy and the emptiness in my life. I was shocked when the doctor said it is cancer, in its very early stages. While I have some time left, I will be joining Annie and Jimmy sooner than I had planned.

What I want more than anything is to see you, Maggie. To know I have family is the only solace and comfort I have at the moment.

I am a fairly wealthy man and can send you the tickets to sail to Ireland as soon as possible. Once you arrive in Queenstown, I will have a driver pick you up and bring you to my home on Ailesbury Road in Dublin.

The political strife in Europe may soon make such travel precarious. You should make the journey as quickly as Eli and your responsibilities with The Ladies from the Hill allow.

Please write and tell me you will come, Maggie.

It is a dying man's wish.

With love and affection from your brother,

James

I long to go see him and write that I will. First, I have to get my life here in order. Eli is becoming increasingly more difficult.

Leon called earlier this week. He has decided to enlist in the Army. I think back to the days when he was happiest playing soldier with a broomstick for a rifle. While I fear for his safety, particularly with what the newspapers and radio report of the aggressive actions of Hitler and his forces, it is a good decision for him.

His father will not agree. As soon as this has settled, I will leave for Ireland.

August

I have made the decision to send Catherine to the Sacred Heart Academy, a boarding school in Buffalo.

Eli's drinking continues to escalate, as do the tensions mounting between the two of us. With Belle gone, I have no one to share my fears and trepidation. The best I can do is to remove Catherine from this toxic environment. Belle's endowment will provide the necessary funds. My heart breaks at the thought of this empty house made even darker by her departure, but it is for the best.

And I am distracted by all the work needed to be done before the house gets remodeled. The kitchen is to be totally refurbished with built-in cabinets and countertops. I will be modern in every way, as Florence likes to point out.

September

We packed Catherine's things last night and drove her to Sacred Heart this morning.

The campus is beautiful, and I said a silent prayer of thanks to Belle for allowing this to happen. The nuns seemed genuinely pleased to have her with them, and we spoke to the Mother Superior about Catherine's dedication to the church choir and her love of music. I am comforted knowing there will be ample opportunity for her to use and develop her talent.

One of the unforeseen blessings of Catherine's move is that both Florence and Walter are tapping into the trust fund to further their own education. Leon has no interest as both he and Louise share Eli's views on the value of education. Instead, Leon called the house last night to say that he will begin basic training in November. Assigned to the infantry, he will be going to Fort Dix in New Jersey. I asked if he was coming home before he leaves. He responded *I'll see* and hung up.

Eli and I are now alone. Or I will be alone, for it has been a long time since I thought of us as a couple. It makes me sad to see how far apart we have become, how our feelings for each other have eroded over time.

But I can change none of that. Not now.

Tomorrow, I will begin planning my trip to Ireland. Having lost Belle, I need to see James. I fear if I don't, I will lose me as well.

I long to see the country I came from. And then I can return to this life with a better understanding of who I am.

There is restlessness in my spirit I believe will be quieted once I have set foot on those shores.

October

I have written to James that I will come after Christmas. His bankers are working with Mr. Harrison to finalize the travel arrangements.

All must be in place before I tell Eli. He will not be pleased, but this is my decision. It is my life. I have given him everything he ever needed and wanted. The children are grown, and Catherine is flourishing at school. It is my turn.

The house is in disarray as the remodeling is going full throttle. Nothing is where it should be or ever was. I don't know how long the chaos will last, but I can barely cook and do the dishes, scavenging for the simplest of pans and essentials. I was not reared to live in this state of confusion, and there is no end in sight.

November

Leon has come home and is staying in Florence's room. He will stay with us until he leaves for the Army before Thanksgiving. He and Eli don't speak; it is as if they are strangers rather than father and son. It breaks my heart–a heart that has been broken so many times I doubt it will ever feel whole again.

I have written to James that all the arrangements for my trip to Ireland have been made. I pray his health will hold out.

I have put the banking in order and have tickets to take the Queen Mary out of New York on January 13, 1937. I return in early March.

The booking agency said that the seas may be rough. I smiled thinking that my Ma and Da probably never got such a warning. Unlike them, I am going in the first-class compartment.

I plan to tell Eli tonight. I am nervous, but since all the arrangements have been made, I can only look forward, not backward. I must return to Ireland. For Ma, for James, and to find a part of me that I lost along the way.

November 22nd

My hand is shaking as I write. I don't know what else to do. Eli hit me. A hard punch that hit the right side of my face and knocked me across the kitchen floor.

I told him I was going to Ireland in January. I didn't ask. He shouted, *No!*

I responded it wasn't his decision to make; it was mine.

He paced around the kitchen, shouting he would do whatever he must to stop me from going. And then I saw a man I had never seen before.

Eli's lips became drawn and strained, his chest pounding so hard that it appeared it might burst, warning of the strike soon to come. His face became contorted; his eyes glazed over like an animal ready to pounce.

I think I now know what it means to be possessed. He told me he was forbidding me to go. I must have infuriated him with whatever answer I gave, for it was then that he hit me. The hands that I had loved, that had held our children, had tilled our soil, flew at my face. I fell to the floor, my head hitting the table. In all the years we have been together, he has never raised his hand to me.

Stunned, I got up slowly. I was angry . . . hot and cold at once, passionately furious and coldly resentful. I looked at him and said, *I leave on the 13th of January. I can either stay in this house until then, or I will go and live with Elizabeth and Ray in Buffalo. It matters not to me.*

He screamed I wouldn't be living anywhere.

Then he grabbed the bottle of whiskey from under the cabinet and slammed the back door shut behind him. I heard him go into the barn, the path lit by the old kerosene lamp he has always used.

For the first time in my life, I am afraid.

There was darkness about him I have never seen before. He will now drink too much and sleep it off in the barn. Tomorrow, in the daylight, we can discuss this as adults. Or I can leave him on his own to fret until he recognizes that my mind will not be changed. It is a choice I hope I will not have to make.

My eye is swelling shut, so I can barely see the page. I have to get up before dawn to make Leon his breakfast. He leaves early to catch the train to take him and the other newly enlisted men to New Jersey. It all seems quite unreal to me.

I am not sure how I can explain the bruises that will be all too visible. I will keep the lights dim so he might not notice.

Eli is back in the house. I hear him stumbling about the kitchen. It is time for me to turn off the light and pray for a better tomorrow.

EPILOGUE

THE DAUGHTER

Do we ever really know our mothers?

They give us birth, feed us, scold us, comfort us and move us on our way. But do we ever listen to them as women? Their secrets, desires, heartbreaks and dreams? Maybe, when their days with us grow shorter.

Mother died before I ever really knew her. It was two days after she made the last entry in this journal.

She was in the kitchen, preparing breakfast for my brother Leon. We were never sure of what happened, but instead of putting cooking oil into the heated pan, she poured kerosene. The pan exploded, and she was ablaze with fire when my brother came into the room.

Mother died the next day of third-degree burns.

With all the commotion, we never found the cooking oil tin. Dad's kerosene lamp was on the table and our one thought was that there had been a mix-up as the cooking oil tin and the kerosene container were of the same shape and size. No one was ever able to piece together how it happened.

We were all at her bedside when the priest came to administer the last rites. Her eyes fluttered opened and her scorched lips mumbled her last, *I love you.*

As she looked at Dad, it sounded like she said, *Forgiven.*

It is hard to remember; even today the emotions are still too raw.

Dad seemed to have no recollection of those horrid days. He was a broken man, white with shock and grief. Days later, he couldn't recall how he had gone for the doctor. It was only the half-burnt kitchen that was the constant reminder of the horror we were living.

At the cemetery, I took his arm and said, *Time to go.*

He yanked his arm away from my hand, shouting: *No! Please, no! This is a nightmare and I must wake up! I never wanted her to leave me. This can't be happening.*

Eventually, we got him back into the house, and he went to his room.

Dad ordered the Celtic cross to be placed on Mother's grave. Walter commented that he had never thought of Mother as being Irish and questioned Dad about his selection. His eyes burned: *She was Irish. Your Mother was Irish. And proud of it. I will hear no more from you.*

And she had a brother, James. Holding up a crumbled telegram, he murmured: *He is dead, too. They are gone. They are all gone.*

As the days and months progressed, Dad seemed to lose heart, to give up on life. He looked different. More rumpled, grayer, thinner, and often smelling of alcohol. With my two brothers gone and only hired hands on the land, the farm began to disintegrate. It was hard to tell if Dad was killing the land or if the land was killing him.

He died in a car accident. They said he had a heart attack, lost control and skidded into the tree. Perhaps. Or perhaps he simply no longer had the energy to live.

He is buried next to Mother and Aunt Belle.

After his passing, it fell to me to clean out the house before putting it up for auction. Mother's things had never been truly packed away. As I was sorting out the last drawer, I found her journals tucked away and hidden under her finest linens.

It has taken me weeks to read and re-read them. I hear her voice on every page. I understand her in death as I never could or would when we were together.

She gave me life, but it is her life I now am part of.

My parting gift to her is to take her journey to Ireland.

1948

Mother's journey to her ancestral home was delayed until the semblance of peace came to Europe. Her journals and her teapot made the move with me from Buffalo to my home just outside New York City. A very different world from the one we grew up in but one, I believe, she would have loved.

On June 8th, I boarded the newly restored Queen Mary for the trip across the Atlantic. It was an easy journey over the seas. I was not prepared, however, for the devastation I saw in London and its surroundings. With all the heartache the War has brought, how lucky and how grateful we must be to have had the battles fought on other lands.

I took the ferry to Dublin and fell in love with the Irish countryside. It reminded me of the farm, with its rolling hills and grazing cows. Dublin was welcoming as I found my way to St. Stephen's Green and the Shelburne Hotel.

Two days later, I had confirmed all the arrangements with the priest at Uncle James's parish. He thought I was quite mad to pay for a burial site and not to bury anyone it. After I explained the story of how my Mother had wanted to return to Ireland but never got the opportunity, he arranged for the plot to be dug and gave me his blessing.

I stood at the shallow grave and placed Mother's teapot in it. I had decided I could not part with the journals. As I finished the last of my prayers and placed a rose on the newly turned ground, I noticed a well-dressed, middle-aged woman staring quite intently at me.

When I was leaving, the woman approached me. In a very distinct American accent she inquired: *May I ask why you are at the Clancy gravesite?*

I replied that James Clancy was my Uncle, and I had come from New York to honor him and pay tribute to my Mother.

Your Mother is from Ireland? She asked.

I said, *yes. But she lived and died in New York.*

She looked at me with eyes that I recognized so well and were now filling up with tears. *You're Maggie's daughter?*

As I nodded yes, she took my hands and pressed them to her heart.

I'm your Aunt Nell.

AUTHOR'S NOTE

The characters in *Becoming Herself* are more fiction than fact. What is true: my maternal grandmother was Margaret George who immigrated from Ireland as a child and was adopted by John & Elizabeth Meyer. She married Eli, lived in Sheldon, New York, was the church organist and died tragically in a kitchen fire in 1936. My mother Eva, her 6th child, remembered the book burning during World War I.

This story was inspired by my grandmother; it is not her memoire. While some of the names are true, all the characters, their virtues and their flaws are products of my imagination. This is a work of fiction and any resemblance to persons living or dead is coincidental.

When it came time to research the history of the time, my reliance on the internet was astounding. Facts about the Easter Uprising in Dublin, the New York Suffragette movement, the hierarchy of hens in the flock, could be researched without ever leaving my office. Having visited

Ireland on several occasions, my memory has a reservoir of tales of the 'little people' and the beauty and unbridled majesty of the Irish coast. You need only to visit this island once to be charmed by its landscape and its people. The same is true of the rolling green hills that grace the Western New York landscape. The harsh winters are softened by the joys that each spring brings. You find resiliency and stalwartness in the people who call upstate their home and can be described as being 'the salt of the earth.' I am proud to have roots in both these lands.

If it takes a village to raise a child, then it takes a community to bring a book into the hands of a reader.

My 'book community' is made up of women, most of whom I have been friends with for so long that I cannot tell you the day we met. I only know that without them, I wouldn't be who I am or where I am. Thank you for taking the time to listen, to critique and to encourage. I am blest to have you— Candi, Carol, Colleen, Erin, Kathy, Louise, Mary Ellen, Sandra, Sandy and Rolaine—in my life. To quote Margaret: *when I am with these women, I can breathe.*

My introduction of what it takes to write, publish and publicize a book was guided by women who are smart, savvy and know the business. Editors Joan Dempsey and Dawna Kempner were encouraging with my manuscript while providing content guidance and grammatical corrections. Publisher Stephanie Larkin of Red Penguin Books took my typed pages and magically turned them into an honest-to-goodness book. Publicist and bookstore owner, Carol Hoenig knows how to get a book and its author noticed. My thanks to you all.

There are no words to express my gratitude to my husband Russ, my partner in this journey called life. Your love fills my heart each and every day. You were the first, the second and sometimes the third reader and aptly assumed the role of time-line checker. With you at my side, everything is possible.

ABOUT THE AUTHOR

Maureen grew up in Western New York, not far from the town that Margaret called home. Having spent her working years managing colleges, corporations and international law firms, she took a deep breath and began her encore career as a consultant to professional service firms.

Becoming Herself is her first novel. She has another story ready to be told.

Maureen lives in the metropolitan New York area. When not traveling with the love-of-her-life, her husband Russ, she spends her time between their home on Long Island and a tiny jewel of a Manhattan apartment overlooking the East River. She is blest that four of the most beautiful, smartest and kindest girls in the world call her "Grandma."

CPSIA information can be obtained
at www.ICGtesting.com
Printed in the USA
LVHW042326070419
613304LV00001B/63/P